For Bob and Bernie Curran

CONTENTS

JOHN Seward is fitting a fresh wax cylinder into his phonograph, preparing to make his usual record of the day's events, when the Principal Attendant of Block 2 bursts through the office door. The night so far has been wasted. He is too preoccupied for work, his thoughts compulsively returning to the events of the previous weekend. How preposterous he must have looked, pacing back and forth across the rug of his sweetheart's drawing room, spilling out his rambling proposal. When she rejected him-tactfully, affectionately-he had lowered himself onto her couch and accidentally crushed his hat. Now, sitting at the mahogany director's desk he worries is too large for his needs, he lifts his spectacles and pinches the bridge of his nose, barely aware of the rain thrumming against the windows. Mr Simmons's unexpected arrival causes him to jolt and bang his knee.

"What the devil is it, man?"

"Renfield has met with an accident, sir. You must come at once."

1

The journey from the Administration Block to the second floor takes only a few minutes, the two men hurrying through the gas lit, black and white tiled corridors and nodding at the night watchers who unlock the doors and allow them to pass. When they reach Renfield's room Seward snaps open the observation hatch. Peering inside he sees rain slanting in through the open sash window and, on the floor near the bed, a crumpled bundle, something like a coal sack. A flash of lightning glances from the surface of a pool of sleek black liquid.

He bangs on the wood with the flat of his hand: "Open up!"

"I think he may have lodged something under the handle," says Mr Simmons.

"Help me."

Together they charge forward, leading with their shoulders. On the third attempt the frame splinters and they break inside, sending a chair clattering across the floor. Light from the corridor reveals the coal sack to be the patient's unmoving body, curled into a loose ball. Taking him by the shoulder Seward rolls him gently onto his back. He is dressed in day clothes, in his navy waistcoat and tie. Below his hairline is a deep wound, most likely the result of a heavy blow from a sharp object. The rest of his face is swollen and distorted, his hair matted with blood.

Mr Simmons fidgets near the doorway: "I think, sir, his

2

back is broken. See, both his right arm and leg and the whole side of his face are paralysed. I can't understand it. He could mark his face like that by beating his own head on the floor. I saw a young woman do it once at the Eversfield Asylum before anyone could lay hands on her. But I can't see how a man could break his own back. And if it was an accident why was the chair pushed up against the door? It doesn't make any sense."

"Who has been in this room since you started your shift?"

"No one, I swear it. I locked the door as usual at nine and haven't opened it since."

"Did you leave your post?"

"No, sir."

A lightning strike announces a thunderclap, the storm passing directly above the madhouse. Catching a sudden gust of wind the wooden window shutter whacks against the wall.

"Listen. I want you to go to Van Helsing and ask him to come here at once. I want him without an instant's delay, do you understand?"

Mr Simmons hurries out, ashen faced and perspiring. Seward carefully rearranges his patient's limbs, taking the pillow from the bed and slipping it under his head. Something falls from Renfield's trouser pocket: a pearl earring. Picking it up Seward balances the shining object in

3

the centre of his palm, studying it with a confused frown before slipping it into his frock coat. Pressing two fingers against the patient's carotid artery he counts the faint throbs: "Poor man."

When Van Helsing arrives his one hand is tucked inside the breast of his dressing gown while his other holds the umbrella that sheltered him on his short trip from the guest's cottage in the grounds. Only his slippers and pyjama bottoms are wet. Mr Simmons follows, soaked to his skin.

"What do we have here then?" says the Dutchman, leaning over the body to give it a cursory visual examination. His uncombed red hair and the crease marks on his cheek betray that he has come straight from his bed. He sniffs decisively-"Allow me to fetch my things"-and leaves.

Crossing his path, Mr Simmons carries a gas lamp from the corridor. After placing it on the floor beside the patient he yanks down the sash window and fastens the shutter. Nothing in the room is out of place. The wardrobe is untouched, the bookshelves undisturbed. A leather-bound critical study of Coleridge's poems rests open on the bedside table.

"And you're certain nobody has been in here?"

"Unless they came in through the window."

"Seems unlikely, no? We're on the second floor." He

looks around the room, stopping when he spots something unusual. "Move the lamp closer to the bed, would you? See, there: on the corner."

Mr Simmons casts the light over a thick clump of greyish pink matter, a deposit of concertinaed skin where Renfield's forehead must have struck the frame: "Christ Almighty."

Violence is to be expected in the life of a madhouse but the Superintendent has not yet lost the capacity to be shocked by it. He has been at Carfax for eight months, transferred from a smaller institution in Edinburgh, but is still overwhelmed by the size of the place: three wings, nine hundred inmates, thirty-five acres: a small, walled town. Carefully, he picks a stray strand of hair from the gash on the patient's forehead. For all his wild misconceptions, Renfield is the most lucid of the inmates and one of the few he senses a kinship with. If this is an attempt at suicide, he should have seen it coming.

Van Helsing returns without his umbrella but bearing a surgical case, his movements unhurried and efficient. Kneeling by the patient he takes a few moments before making an assessment, the whisky he drank before bed still evident on his breath. Seward studies his former teacher from the corner of his eyes: the compressed line of his mouth, his sculptured forehead and the small tufts of red hair in his nostrils.

"The facial wounds are superficial," he says. "Our real concern here is a depressed fracture of the skull. We must reduce the pressure of the swelling and get back to normal conditions, as far as can be. The whole motor area seems affected. The suffusion of the brain will increase quickly, so we must trephine at once or it may be too late."

Two men appear in the doorway, dripping wet: Doctor Godalming and Seward's American friend Quincey Morris. Godalming wears a greatcoat over his nightgown. His companion is fully dressed: "I heard your man call up Doctor Van Helsing and tell him of the incident. Is there anything we can do to help?"

Beckoning them inside Seward asks if they would close the door. A tiny reddish spider descends from the ceiling on an invisible thread. Godalming waves it away from his face.

"What happened?" asks Morris, his Texan drawl still strong after a decade in England. "Jesus."

"Mr Renfield appears to have been attempting to bash his brains out using the bed frame," replies Seward, "apparently with some success. I don't know. I can't see how his injuries could be self-inflicted."

Van Helsing has removed the trephine from his case and is testing the mechanism, watching the circular saw rotate in the gas light: "There is no time to lose," he says, although little urgency is relayed by his measured tone.

"The haemorrhage is increasing. We will operate above the ear."

On seeing the spike at the centre of the blade pierce Renfield's skin, Mr Simmons blanches: "Doctor Seward, sir, may I be allowed to leave the room?"

"Of course."

Morris leans against the wall and observes, pulling at the corners of his moustache. Godalming retrieves the fallen chair, the rain still shining on his bald scalp. Turning the trephine's handle Van Helsing slices a circle from the patient's swollen flesh, causing the clot to burst and spill forth, rushing over his ear and soaking the pillow cover. Immediately Renfield opens his eyes and blinks, struggling to comprehend his surroundings.

"What's wrong with my face?" His speech is imprecise, the words twisting clumsily from the left side of his mouth: "I have had an awful dream."

"Try not to move."

He recognises the accent, and it pleases him: "That is Doctor Van Helsing."

"Tell us what your dream was about," says the surgeon, hoping to focus the patient's mind and distract him from his injuries.

"Give me some water, my lips are dry."

Seward asks Morris to run and fetch some brandy. Closing his eyes Renfield takes a breath and lifts his right hand to his face, using his fingertips to explore its altered contours. When he comes near the raw wound below his hairline he shivers in pain. Morris returns carrying a decanter of spirits, a carafe of water, and a glass.

Van Helsing wets Renfield's lips: "Your dream. Tell us about it."

Using Seward's eyes as a focal point the patient struggles to gather his thoughts: "Seward."

"Yes."

"I don't feel at all well."

"I know."

"This is the end, isn't it?"

"Absolutely not."

"I wish I could have been more like you, Seward. I wish I could have been a better man. But I never had a chance. My path was set from the beginning. I have done unforgivable things. But I have tried to make amends. You must believe it." He swallows dryly, thinking hard. "I have had an awful dream... No, I must not deceive myself... I have something to tell you, before it is too late."

"We may save you yet, Renfield."

"Please, let me continue. I heard dogs barking beyond the grounds..." Sleepily he rambles, his voice growing ever weaker, his pronunciation increasingly slurred. The fantasy he relates is dislocated and bizarre, of a woman obscured by a whirl of blossoms, of a fierce black hound spitting hot drool, of a man with feline teeth and shiny pebbles in place of eyes. Of dirt, trees and blood and a bloated figure tapping on the window.

Van Helsing dips his handkerchief into the carafe and wrings out the excess before running it gently over the patient's misshaped and tender face, letting him speak. The gas light casts flickering shadows across the ceiling. Nobody is listening.

PART ONE

Green Tea

FIRST came the constant weariness, as if my sleep had been disturbed.

I seldom altered my nightly customs. At eleven the hallway clock would strike and I would rise from the bureau at which I carried out my duties as the editor of *The Mind* to move my candle to the bedroom and disrobe by its light. Invariably my nightclothes would be where I left them the previous morning: my gown folded beneath my pillow along with a pair of thick woollen socks to keep my feet warm. Once undressed I would hang my suit in the wardrobe. I owned four in all, each identical, purchased over a period of years from the same Devonshire tailor, consisting of a braided navy blue frock coat, a high buttoned waistcoat, narrow cut trousers and a lilac speckled tie. My boots went by the door. Lastly I would perform my exercises and climb into bed, extinguishing my candle with a brass snuffer. I slept as I had since I was a child, as my uncle taught me: my arms by my sides and my palms down flat on the mattress. At five thirty I rose again, for many years a deep and dreamless sleeper.

The change came without warning. Accustomed to

feeling energetic and mentally alert during the day I found myself experiencing periods of lassitude and melancholy, suffering irritating mouth ulcers and aches in my limbs. A dull pain around the temples was my constant companion. Aside from these minor ailments, though, I could complain of no bodily derangement and so, observing myself with a physician's eye, concluded my condition was one of the imagination and would soon pass.

Next came the insomnia itself. Waking suddenly into the gross darkness of my room I would find it impossible to return to sleep. With my spine straight and my fingers together I listened to the unfamiliar noises of the house at night: the knocking of the pipes, the creaking walls, moths tapping against the ceiling. Often I would abandon any hope of drifting off and try instead to occupy my mind, reigniting the candle and picking up the well-thumbed editions of Wordsworth's *The Prelude* or Goethe's *Die Laiden des Jungen Werthers* I inherited from my old childhood acquaintance, Oscar. Yet despite my wakefulness I was unable to make much sense of anything I read and was reduced to running my eyes uncomprehendingly over sentences again and again. Ultimately it proved less frustrating to remain still and pray for sleep to find me.

What little rest I was granted came accompanied by dreams so shapeless and obscure that I could seldom recall them, but which left me with a sense of great exhaustion, as if I had survived a period of intense mental effort. By the morning only the memory of a voice remained, speaking at a vast distance and bringing forth muddled feelings of fear, regret and shame.

I mentioned all this to David Toynbee when he made his regular Thursday evening visit to my home.

"I'm sure it's nothing serious," he said, having already commented on the dark rings around my eyes. "Have you made any changes to your diet recently?"

He was planted in his usual chair in my drawing room, one long leg dangling over the other and occasionally nudging against the low table which stood between us whenever he grew animated. My friend was possessed of the most singular features: a hooked nose, a tapered chin and unruly red hair that proved invulnerable to even the most generous application of Macassar oil. His eyebrows were arched in a way that gave him the appearance of being eternally astonished.

"Not that I can think of. I may have been consuming more green tea than usual."

One of his remarkable eyebrows rose at this: "Green tea? Really?" Picking up his decanter he filled his wine glass for the third time, his movements suggesting a frantic nervous impatience despite him being perfectly relaxed. "How funny you should say that. Have you ever heard of Martin Emerson?"

"Should I have? Is he a medical man?"

"Absolutely not, although he's certainly quick to describe himself as a doctor. I came across him when I was staying in New York, in the dining room of the Hotel Chelsea."

For much of the previous year David had been touring the United States with his family, making a study of their lunatic asylums. On his return he was full of disturbing reports of retrogressive behaviour by our American counterparts, of the mistreatment of patients and the systematic overuse of mechanical restraints. But try as he might, he could not conceal how much pleasure he had taken in the trip. More than once he had stated his desire to move there with his family, where he had a sense of something new being created, something thrilling. He longed to leave the fog and drizzle of London behind: the great city had, in his opinion, entered a state of terminal decline.

"He makes his living giving what he calls 'trance lectures', where he claims to commune with spirits. We got along rather well so he invited me and Sarah to one of his performances at Union Hall. It was quite the spectacle. His trick is to encourage the audience to suggest difficult topics—when I was there, for example, people proposed primitive rocks, evolution theory and, I think, the Neapolitan War—then proceed to speak on them at length

16

and in impressive detail. His seemingly boundless knowledge, he suggests, is imparted to him by a band of ghosts who bring him information from the other side."

"A very diverting piece of theatre, I'm sure, but what does all this have to do with my diet?"

"I'm getting to that. It is his assertion, both on stage and off, that humans possess a kind of sixth sense, something he calls 'interior vision', quite distinct from ordinary 'exterior vision'. Rather than being situated in the eyes, it is located immediately about and above the eyebrows, in the nervous tissue of the brain." He tapped his forefinger against his temple. "Learning how to use it gives a person insight into a non-corporeal world which exists parallel to our own: the domain of angels and demons, an entire unseen realm. This extra sense, usually dormant, can be awakened in a variety of ways, using meditation for example, or prayer, or extended periods of solitude. It can also be awoken in error, through various abuses, the chief of which, he says, in the overconsumption of green tea."

"So if you take what he says to be true then my bad dreams are, in fact, glimpses into another world?"

"It might explain why you seldom remember them: because your waking mind is incapable of processing the non-sensual."

"You'll forgive me for saying this all sounds rather

unlikely."

"Yes, I'll grant you that." He smiled self-indulgently and took another sip of Amontillado. "No doubt the man is a charlatan. But when he's in the footlights I must admit he can be highly persuasive. He talks of a whole new world, an unknown Earth. When he's getting particularly carried away he swears blind he has seen the Apocalypse, although he prefers to call it 'The Renewal'. It's coming soon, he says. Society is collapsing. Civilization is on the brink of a catastrophe. We are living in the *end of days*. You can see why so many people flock to watch him perform. It's made him a very wealthy man."

The evening over, we exchanged our farewells and I made my way to the study to sketch out some cursory notes on an article I have been writing for *The Mind*, on the advantages of excessive feeding in the treatment of certain cases of neurasthenia and hysteria. Before long the hallway clock had struck eleven and it was time for me to perform my exercises then – with some trepidation – to go to bed, administering myself a mild barbiturate before I did so.

The Feast of Roses

I had always set the greatest store by an energetic morning walk. The fresh air combined with steady rhythm of my steps seldom failed to leave me feeling ready for the challenges of the coming day. This was never truer than in the rural surroundings of Devon County Asylum. For thirteen years I held the position of Medical Superintendent, an activity which while bringing with it constant tensions and setbacks-as tragically demonstrated by the suicide of my long-time acquaintance Doctor Finch at Brislington House-I took great satisfaction in performing. Each morning before my working day commenced, regardless of the weather, I would leave the accommodation I kept in the grounds and head in the direction of the airing court, from where I would pace at speed along the outer perimeter and through the orchard, rounding the nearby farmer's fields and finally bringing my journey to an end at the great door of the main building. When I moved to Marylebone I sought the same sense of solitude and briskness in Regent's Park, only a short distance from my home. Although it was almost impossible to ever be truly alone amongst London's multitudes, this routine at least provided me with the chance to invigorate my body and order my thoughts.

On entering the park via Chester Terrace that morning I found it markedly busier than I would usually expect, lively with people of all ages dressed as if for a special event. Approaching the Royal Botanic Gardens I happened across a stationary row of coaches brightly decorated with red roses. A marquee was in the process of being erected on a nearby stretch of grass and multicoloured paper lamps were being hung in the trees. Asking a nearby woman the purpose of all this I was informed that preparations were being made for something called The Feast of Roses, a parade due to take place later that afternoon. Thanking her I changed direction and took my handkerchief from my top pocket. Already my hay fever was beginning to bother me. A man with daffodils poking out of his top hat walked by: judging by his expression he was greatly amused by his own appearance.

Leaving the hubbub behind I spotted a tall young woman coming towards me from the direction of Saint Catherine's Lodge, attractively dressed in a plain gored skirt and a masculine tie, her hair tied beneath a straw sailor hat. With one hand she was pushing a perambulator while the other supported a white parasol, the handle of which rested on her shoulder. I was quite taken by her remarkable looks and found I had to resist the urge to stare: something that had not happened to me for many years, physical beauty having long ago lost its hold over me.

As we drew level the wind gathered strength and surged into a sustained burst, threatening to tear the parasol from her. A second gust turned the shade inside out. Seeing she was battling to keep hold of it while also preventing the pram from rolling away I naturally stepped in to provide assistance. No sooner had I grasped the crook handle, however, than it was pulled from my fingers. Together we watched it bounce and scrape along the gravel, making its way towards one of the park's many ornate fountains. Setting after it I left my business bag with the young woman, walking at speed but unwilling to embarrass myself by breaking into a run. With dismay I saw the contraption lift over the edge of the basin and tumble into the water. Arriving at the fountain's edge I reached for it using the full extent of my arm but only managed to push it farther away. It was clear I was going to have to climb onto the stone rim. For balance, I held my arms out to my sides, the tails of my frock coat flapping wildly about my legs.

"Please don't trouble yourself so," said the lady, who had moved the pram over to me.

To reassure her I was happy to help I raised my hand—it was, after all, my fault the parasol had ended up where it was—but put it instantly down when I began to lose my equilibrium. Twice I feared I would spill headlong into the

21

water but, thankfully, I managed to suffer nothing worse than a soaked boot. It was sheer luck that the wind changed direction and delivered the handle to my waiting hand. My dismount was less than elegant.

The woman offered her thanks. She was almost the same height as me, with blue-green eyes and a proud young face. Behind her, pink and white blossoms whirled across the pathway, shaken from the trees, while two muscular black mares trotted slowly by: "I really am extremely grateful."

I shook the water from the shade and sheepishly handed it back.

Again, she thanked me: "You are very kind."

"Not at all. It is a pleasure. I only hope it isn't damaged beyond repair."

"I wish there were some reward I could offer you."

"No, no. That I could be of any assistance at all, however small, is reward enough…. Well. Good day to you."

"Good day, sir."

Once we had parted company I checked my watch. Time had gotten away from me. My right boot squelching, I set off for my appointment in Wandsworth. It was far later than I had imagined.

Mr Utterson's Room

"I was most encouraged by your letter. From what you say I think it would not be irresponsible to suggest your husband may yet make a full recovery."

I had recently arrived at the Utterson residence, having been met by their landau at Wandsworth Station and taken on the short journey to their detached villa. On opening the garden gate I was greeted by a grey kitten that rubbed insistently against my ankles, pestering me to be stroked. Lifting its body up with the end of my boot–now mercifully dry–I moved it out of my way.

At the door I was greeted by a butler of extraordinary girth, who led me with wheezing breaths through a high-roofed hall paved with flags and into the drawing room, where the lady of the house was waiting. I would never normally have considered visiting a private patient but Mrs Utterson had written to me on the advice of an old colleague from Devon, so I felt unable to refuse. I did not intend to waste much time over the matter.

She replied to my statement uncertainly, staring at her large, freckled hands where they rested in her lap: "It saddens me to tell you that things have changed since I wrote those words."

We were sat on a Chesterfield running parallel to a large bay window, behind a low table on which were displayed several copies of *Penny Magazine*. An enormous and plump-leafed rubber plant dominated the corner nearest the door. Glancing about the room I felt satisfied the family's decision to take Mr Utterson out of Highgate Infirmary had been the correct one. A person accustomed to these rich surroundings could only suffer in that institution's stark and impersonal wards, whatever my less enlightened peers might say about the shortcomings of domestic care.

Mrs Utterson was woman in her thirtieth year, thickset with salt-and-pepper hair and prim, puckered lips. A prominent black mole spoiled the line of her chin. Despite her sitting bolt upright with her round shoulders placed firmly back, her fatigue betrayed itself in her pallor.

"He has been in very low spirits. He had been progressing so excellently since he came home: venturing out of his room, even sharing a meal or two with me. Privately I had begun to hope he would soon be returned to his former self. Now, without warning, he has retreated once more. It is almost as if we never sought help at all."

"Have you any idea what might have triggered this setback?"

"I only wish I could say. I cannot make sense of his behaviour. He locks himself away all day and night, refusing to speak to the servants. His attitude towards me is ill-tempered and dismissive. He cannot bring himself to look me in the eye."

"And how long has this been going on for?"

Covering her face, she began to cry. Waiting for her to collect herself I took the opportunity to examine a painting that hung over the fireplace, depicting a location I was certain I recognised but was unable to place: a packhorse bridge over a quiet river, backgrounded by trees.

"It has been difficult for me also, Doctor Renfield," she said at last, when she had regained her composure.

"I understand."

"Since my husband was forced to give up his legal practice life has been nothing but a struggle for us. It is only a matter of time before our savings run out. The servants are unhappy working in such an environment, with their employer nowhere to be seen. I worry they will seek alternative employment and leave me unable to find replacements. People on the street stare at me, Doctor Renfield. They are cold and unkind. They must know what has befallen us. It is barely tolerable."

My attention was again drawn by the painting. It irritated me that I could not place the scene. Pulling myself away from this distraction I addressed the matter at hand: "In my experience, which I can assure you is considerable, those suffering from melancholia are often prone to setbacks. These relapses can be distressing and disheartening, but they are also transitory. We must not let them waylay us."

It was decided we should go upstairs to see the patient. Mr Utterson's room was situated on the third floor, at the end of a long corridor lined with what seemed to me to be an excessive number of flower bouquets. The lady of the house led the way, hesitating at the door before giving it a gentle knock. The sound of hurried movement came from within: a chair sliding across the floor, a drawer pushed closed, followed by Mr Utterson's voice: "Is that you, May?"

"Yes, Charles. Doctor Renfield is with me. Please unlock the door; he has come to see you."

"I will not be receiving visitors today."

I kept my voice low to prevent the occupant from hearing: "How is he able to lock the door?"

"He has a key."

"This must be taken from him as soon as possible. It could be dangerous. Explain that he may close the door if he wishes, but it must remain unlocked at all times."

Something brushed against my trouser leg. Looking down I saw the grey kitten from the front garden, vying again for my attention.

Mrs Utterson gave another knock: "He has come all the way from Marylebone. You remember I mentioned he would come?"

"Of course I remember. Kindly stop talking to me as if I'm a child."

"Please, Charles. He has come a long way."

"Then I'm afraid he has wasted his time."

"Don't embarrass me, please. Open the door."

After a few moments the key turns in the lock.

The kitten entered before me. Inside the air was tropically hot and pungent with cigar smoke. Thick green velvet curtains were drawn over the window, starving everything of sunlight. Evidently the room, now containing an unmade bed, had once served as a study. Two of the walls were lined with shelves crammed with books. Opposite the window hung a sombre piece of tapestry representing Cleopatra cradling an asp, beneath which sat an ornate writing desk. A cheroot smouldered in its ashtray.

His back half turned to us, the man of the house made a show of trying to locate some misplaced volume. Even at first glance it was obvious he was a person who placed no particular value on physical robustness, what with his underdeveloped limbs, greyish complexion and pronounced pot belly. I cast an eye across the shelf where he stood, displaying a selection of texts with which I was familiar—Percy, Chatterton, and Burger—along with a title I did not recognise: *Arcana Caelestia* by Emmanuel Swedenborg.

I asked Mrs Utterson if she would leave us alone.

"Certainly," she replied. "I will wait for you downstairs."

The lawyer continued his search as if oblivious to my presence. Taking a position in the centre of the room I asked why he did not open the curtains.

"I am perfectly happy as I am," came the quietly spoken reply. Moving a few steps along the shelves he lifted his hand to select something, and then thought better of it. I placed a finger under my nostrils to block out the stale stench of countless cigars, understanding now why the corridor outside contained such an abundance of strongly scented flowers. The ceiling and the tops of the walls were tobacco stained, a yellowish colour like a London fog.

"Do you not find it difficult to read in so little light?"

"I much prefer it this way. It helps me concentrate."

"You'll strain your eyes. Besides, it does no good to surround yourself in gloom."

Mr Utterson put his hands behind his back and looked down at the floor. "Honestly, Doctor Renfield, we both know you're only here out of a sense of obligation. Is all this necessary? You are keeping me from my studies."

Reaching over the makeshift bed I pulled the curtains open, tugging at the hooks where they stuck along the track.

"Doctor Renfield!"

"'Do you not know that your bodies are
Spirit, who is in you, whom you have received fro.
your own; you were bought at a price. Therefor
your bodies. First Corinthians, but I'm sure y
that. Open the windows. Move around. Take some air."

The kitten emerged from the crumpled bedding, mewing pathetically. Dust motes spun in the sunlight. Mr Utterson, I realised, had been using his theatrical search for a book to move farther away from me, towards the corner of the room. Shielding his eyes he muttered something under his breath. Ignoring it I asked what subject he was studying.

"You wouldn't understand."

"You would do well not to underestimate me, sir."

"It's not a question of underestimating you. I am taking steps into a unique field of science, something completely new. Comprehending even the smallest part of it would require years of deep and diligent reading."

"What kind of science?"

"There's no point in attempting to put it into words, and even if I thought I could describe the concept in a way that you could grasp, I still wouldn't share it. The whole thing is too dangerous and demands to be handled with the greatest of care. It changes everything. It changes the way we see man's place in the universe. All I can tell you for sure is that everything you currently believe is wrong."

of curiosity I stepped forward and plucked *Arcana*
.lestia from its place in the centre of the row. It was a
fine edition, bound in a natty livery, with its pages
separated here and there by torn slips of paper. I opened it
at one of the marked passages. The text was in Latin but I
was able to translate a few lines without much trouble:
"When a man's interior sight is opened, which is that of his spirit,
then there appear things of another life, which cannot possibly be
made visible to the bodily sight…"

All at once I became disagreeably light-headed and
queasy, no doubt a result of breathing in the thickly
polluted air. Replacing the book, I thanked Mr Utterson
for his time and hurried out with the kitten trotting along
beside me. As soon as I crossed the threshold I heard the
rumble of footsteps and the door slammed shut. Pausing
for a moment I filled my lungs with the cleansing aroma
of the flowers before heading down the stairs.

When I reached the first floor I became aware of a
faint clicking sound coming from behind a door that had
been left slightly ajar, as if someone was snapping their
fingers to draw my attention. I was, of course, somewhat
reluctant to investigate further, fearful of intruding on
some private domestic scene. However the thought struck
me that this, perhaps, was where Mrs Utterson meant
when she told me she would be waiting 'downstairs'.
Receiving no reply when I knocked, I pushed the door

slowly open. To my astonishment, I found the elegantly decorated bedroom to be silent and unoccupied. I pulled the door closed and continued down the stairs.

Mrs Utterson was waiting for me in the hallway on the ground floor.

"Remove his books," I told her. "His fixation with them is unhealthy. Their presence aggravates his condition. And ensure his windows are kept open for at least a few hours a day. The fresh air will do him good."

She looked disappointed: "Is that all you can advise?"

"For the moment, yes. Trust me, it will help. I am an expert."

Leaving the house I declined the use of the landau and chose to make my way to the station on foot, hoping to rid my clothes of the stink of stale tobacco.

Magdalene in the Trees

JOURNEYING home to Marylebone I shared my train carriage with a wispy-haired gentleman who attempted to engage me in conversation. Stuttering over every second word he struggled his way through predictable comments on the expense of his ticket, the unseasonable weather, the women's suffrage movement. After providing a few cursory replies I took my copy of the *Pall Mall Gazette* from my bag and hid myself behind its open pages, trying to concentrate on its contents but finding myself unable to do so. My thoughts continued to be taken up by the landscape painting that hung above the Utterson's mantle. Why was I unable to place the location?

I had been staring blankly at the newspaper for a matter of minutes when the answer finally came to me: it was a depiction of an old stone bridge that spanned a narrow stretch of the River Esk, a few miles from the house I had shared with my uncle from the age of twelve. While it was true the painting was somewhat clumsily executed I was nonetheless amazed it took me so long to recognise the subject. I had spent more days there than I could count.

On these summer trips I was invariably accompanied

by my uncle's friend Oscar and his daughter Magdalene, a girl roughly the same age as I with dark eyes and wavy black hair. After picking me up from my house in the mid-morning the three of us would travel together in their family's coach to our favourite secluded spot. It was a journey I could still recall decades later, with undimmed clarity: Magdalene by my side, Oscar sitting opposite us and fiddling with his enormous beard, the horse's hooves clopping against the track ahead. It was our habit to list the familiar landmarks as they passed the window: a red pillar box, a small village shop displaying jars of sweets, a row of cottages painted a brilliant white. Part of the road wound along the crest of a deep valley, giving us a spectacular view of a dense wood on the far side. All of this still felt new to me, having spent most of my life up to this point in the missionary settlement in Ceylon, and the countryside of Yorkshire seemed almost impossibly beautiful.

Our imminent arrival at our destination was signalled by a sudden downward slope, steep enough for me to quietly take hold of the door handle in fear of the horses losing control and tipping the coach over. At the foot of the hill we disembarked and climbed over a fence stile, leaving our vehicle behind to cross the grassy field and lay out our picnic.

The river at this point was somewhat narrow, thirty feet

wide at the most, with steep bare banks. The bridge spanning it was at least a few hundred years old, its moss covered path leading from the field over to woodland on the other side. It was Oscar's preference—while Magdalene and I paddled or skimmed stones-to stretch his huge legs out in the long grass and flick through whatever books he had bought with him. Sometimes he would call us to his side and read aloud from a passage that he found particularly stirring. The headmaster of a small school for day boys, he was an educator by inclination as well as by profession. What I remember most vividly about him is his smell: his smell, and his enormous beard. It was as if he had passed so many days in libraries that the dusty, musty odour of the paper had permanently permeated his skin, as indelibly as a tattoo.

One burning and muggy afternoon I recall he drifted into a comfortable slumber on the blanket while Magdalene and I picked quietly at the grass by the riverside. I had fallen into a preoccupied mood that I seemed unable to shake despite my best efforts: I had been greatly looking forward to the trip and was annoyed with myself for being incapable of enjoying it. Evidently Magdalene found my lack of engagement equally frustrating: "Why are you being so boring today?"

It shocked me to hear her speak so abruptly, especially within earshot of an adult, even if he was sleeping one.

When we first met she had been reluctant to speak at all, hiding behind her father and keeping her voice low. Now she was changing, growing in confidence. When we were alone together she was capable of becoming quite domineering.

Too proud to admit she was right–I *was* being boring–I stared at the clumps of grass in my hands, pretending I had not heard.

"Let's do something," she said. "Let's go paddling."

Keen to kill my despondency, I suppressed my instincts and agreed. Climbing down the steep bank we supported ourselves by resting our hands against the bridge's masonry then removed our shoes at the river's edge. At first the water was breathtakingly cold but we soon became accustomed to it. On our last visit we had discovered that if we stayed still for long enough translucent minnows moved in to dart around our feet and nip testingly at our toes. Magdalene observed them keenly with her blue-grey eyes. I, in turn, observed her, not because I harboured any feelings beyond friendship, but out of sheer curiosity. I was fascinated by the way she held herself, her unguarded expressions. She was the only girl I knew.

"I'm tired of this," she said, startling me with one of the sudden shifts in mood which were becoming characteristic of her. "Let's go into the woods."

I glanced over to where Oscar was lying. From our

position all I could see of him were the tips of his shoes poking out above the grass: "Are you sure that's a good idea?"

We had never crossed the bridge before and I was uncertain whether it would be permitted. Looking back at my friend I saw her face had undergone a swift transformation: her teeth were gritted, her brow furrowed. Down by her side her hands were tightly clenched.

"If you don't come with me," she said with some intensity, "I will go on my own."

We stepped out of the water and dried our feet on the grass at the top of the slope. Halfway over the river I looked behind me again, fascinated to see such a familiar scene from an unfamiliar angle. Oscar was still fast asleep, his hands resting on his chest and his rib cage moving slowly up and down.

As we passed through the line of trees on the other side of the bridge the temperature dropped, encouraging in me a feeling of portentousness. To our right an overgrown and ill-defined path wound away and was lost to sight amid the thickening trees. Clouds of midges hung in the air. An unwelcome memory came to me of a story I heard in Ceylon, concerning a man who had met the devil in a forest and been tricked into surrendering his soul. Above us a canopy of branches cast a steady shadow, unmoved by any breeze.

Magdalene's anger dissipated as quickly as it appeared. Setting off down the track she smiled to herself and removed her hat: a relaxed attitude that helped to assuage my fears. Idly she asked if I knew the species of the trees around us and I jumped on the chance to show off my knowledge.

"The ones along the river bank are Common Alders," I said, trying to conceal my excitement by controlling my breathing. "These are Fraxinus excelsior, although you probably know them as Ash trees. Those plants by your feet are Hosta, I think. I'm fairly sure that's correct."

"How do you know? Do they teach that at your school?"

I was delighted at what I took to be an acknowledgement of my expertise: "No, I read a few books."

Reaching a deep ravine we stopped at a tree with a broad trunk, against which Magdalene rested. At the bottom of the sharp drop ran a path of jagged rocks, glistening with water. One of my trouser legs, I noticed, had become snagged on a thorn. I removed it carefully to avoid tearing the material. A cloud had passed over the sun, causing my irrational worries to resurface.

"We should go soon. In case Oscar wakes up and wonders where we are."

In response to my caution Magdalene merely shrugged then, with renewed energy, sprang forward and ran deeper into the wood, skipping to avoid a nettle patch. To my relief she came to a halt after only a few seconds: it seemed she had spotted something on the ground a few feet ahead: "I wonder how it died?"

On the lip of a shallow ditch a recently deceased animal lay on a damp patch of soil: a hare, flopped on its back, half eaten with its eyes missing and its guts exposed.

"Poke it."

"No!"

"Go on!" She picked up a stick and offered it to me. Reluctantly I accepted it and stepped forward. Pressing the tip against the hare's hind leg made me nauseated, although I tried my best not to show it. Something in the way the creature's body was splayed struck me as obscene.

"What's been eating it, do you think?"

"A fox, maybe?" I said. "Or a wild dog?"

"You don't really think wild dogs live around here, do you?"

Seeing a chance to encourage her to leave I said that yes, I thought they probably did. My effort made little difference.

"See if you can pick it up."

"It's too heavy."

"At least try!"

Blocking my nose for fear of any smell the corpse might emit I managed to slip the stick under its hindquarters. Flipping it on its side revealed a squirming ball of fat white maggots. Magdalene's exclamations of disgust contradicted the look of wonder in her eyes.

"Come on," she said finally. "Let's go."

On our way out of the wood she broke a period of silence to ask if I was afraid to die.

"No," I replied. In truth I had never given the matter any thought.

"Nonsense, of course you're afraid. Everyone is…. Your mother died, didn't she?"

"Yes, but it was a very long time ago. I don't remember much about her."

"My mother died too. I still miss her. But I think daddy misses her more. What do you think happens after we're gone? Do we go to heaven?"

The question confused me. The answer seemed so obvious that it was barely worth addressing, like asking if the sky was blue or the grass was green: "If we've been good, of course we do. Where else would we go?"

Without answering she skipped up onto the side of a fallen ash tree and reached out her hand to help me up. Thick, fleshy fungus with caps the size of dinner plates grew on the underside of the trunk. Once we were safely on the ground again I tried to release my grip but my friend refused. We walked like this, our fingers wound together, until we were back at the bridge.

I was awakened from these reminiscences by the stuttering old man opposite me in the carriage, asking me where I was travelling to. It was as he faltered over the 't' for the fourth time over that I lost my patience and interrupted.

"What possible b-b-business could that be of yours?"

Casting me a wounded look he gathered his things and went into the corridor without a word. Looking out at the passing tenements I ran my tongue searchingly over the swollen ulcer on the inside of my bottom lip.

The Visitor in Lunacy

HAVING measured the width of the subject's jaw line using a pair of steel callipers, Doctor Monastero set about carefully arranging the electrical conductors around her face. Roughly the shape and size of cigars and mounted on metal stands of varying heights, they were attached to trailing wires which disappeared behind a Chinese silk screen. Once satisfied with his work the elderly Italian limped back to his camera and evaluated the composition with a thin-lipped frown.

Seated at the centre of the scene was a woman in a loose white gown and a shawl, her hair scraped away from her face in a severe ponytail. Two of the copper conductors touched against her eyebrows, two more had been placed on her cheeks. Buckled brown leather straps bound her wrists to the armrests of her chair while another, broader strap around her neck helped keep her head upright and steady. Only the whites of her eyes were showing, her pupils having rolled up beneath their lids.

Monastero's assistant—a bear-like German with a swallow-tailed beard—looked up from his notebook and suggested in flawless English that the room should be made a shade darker. With a shallow nod of agreement the doctor asked for the curtains to be partly drawn. We were on the ground floor of Sutton Asylum, overlooking over the gardens. Four small circular impressions remained on the carpet where the billiard table had been hauled out to make way for the photography studio. An empty cue rack rung on the wall.

The light sufficiently dimmed, Monastero gestured with his liver-spotted hands. His frame, diminished by age, was too small for his immaculate frock coat and his sleeves hung low over his wrists. Responding to the command the German dropped his pencil smartly into the pocket of his brightly coloured waistcoat and stepped behind the screen.

"Number four. Strong stimulation of zygotmaticus major and corrugator supercilli."

All at once the subject's countenance was transformed. Deep creases cut across her forehead and her mouth turned down sharply at the corners. She was like a gargoyle, her features becoming exaggerated and grotesque while her eyes remained as lifeless as stone.

Monastero took the photograph and replaced the lens cap. As the humming of the generator died away the woman's expression collapsed.

"So you see, gentlemen, combine the muscles associated with joy and pain at certain degrees of contraction and you will produce a grimace."

"So it would seem." I blinked away the residual light

from the flash lamp and waved at the smoke. My hay fever was nettlesome enough without this additional irritation.

Superintendent Godalming grinned from the chair next to me, the light at his back glowing red through his jug-handle ears: "Fantastic," he said. "Fascinating."

I asked him when I might be allowed to continue with my inspection.

"Soon, Doctor Renfield, soon. You'll want to hear the rest of this. Do go on, Doctor Monastero."

With a nod the Italian continued with his presentation: "The human face has five primary expressions: joy, misery, pain, pleasure and fear. Combinations of these five basic arrangements allow us to exhibit more complex emotions: restrained jubilation, for example, or embarrassment, or regret. If we activate them properly, as if by the spirit, the facial muscles respond in characteristic patterns, allowing them to be documented and classified."

Monastero had taken short-term residence in the asylum and been given his pick of the inmates to use as subjects in his studies. Godalming, it seemed, considered this work to be of unparalleled significance. I had been partway through my tour of the institution when he took me by the arm and insisted I be given a demonstration.

"It is my hope," said the Italian, "this photographic collection will be of practical use not only to physicians in diagnosing a patient's state of mind, but also to artists.

What better way to learn how to correctly render an emotion on the human face?"

While he spoke the German was busy consulting his notebook and rearranging the conductors. A spot of drool appeared on the inmate's bottom lip, which he distractedly wiped away using the pad of his thumb.

"Consider the sensation of love. The difference between the expression of terrestrial love and the more sublime expression of celestial love is only slight, and something which artists have frequently failed to appreciate. Bernini's sculpture in the church of Saint Maria della Vittoria, for example, depicts Saint Theresa in what appears to be a state of base sensual pleasure rather than what we must presume the artist intended: Christian rapture. Her eyes are half closed, her lips are full and parted. The image verges on the obscene. In my own work, using only electrical pulses, I have been able to produce representations of a far purer joy. The joy of a soul devoted to a higher being."

Confident the subject was sufficiently sedated and posed no threat, the German unfastened her straps and crossed her hands over her chest. After pulling her shawl up over her hair he once again concealed himself behind the silk screen.

Monastero approached his subject and, with the deftness of a conjurer, produced a silver necklace from his coat pocket: "This," he said, placing it around her neck, "is the ideal poetry of human love."

Taking the sound of the generator as his cue he stepped aside to reveal the woman's suddenly altered features: her raised mouth, her widened eyes, her tightened skin. She looked exalted, rapturous. On her chest the silver cross flashed in a beam of sunlight.

I took out my handkerchief and blew my nose: "Doctor? May we? Time is short."

Godalming relented: "Let's get on with it then."

I was led to Block 6, which housed the inmates considered to pose the highest risk to themselves as well as others: the violent, the suicidal, and the epileptic. As was befitting an area of this type in a hospital for the criminally insane, the corridors were prison-like and heavily staffed, the walls featureless and grey. Somewhere in the grounds the peafowl were calling to each other. Selecting a padded cell I asked to be allowed inside.

"I presume you are able to provide me with a satisfactory justification for Mr Arscott's restraints?"

The patient was balled up at the foot of the wall adjacent to the doorway, his tense figure strapped into straight waistcoat made of duck cloth.

"Of course," said Godalming. "He has cast the attendants as his enemies and feels compelled to defend

45

himself. Mark my words, if I were to remove his jacket he would attack as soon as the final buckle was loosened. Mr O'Conner will testify to that."

The young attendant guarding the door lifted the peak of his cap to show off his black eye.

"Do you administer surprise baths as part of his treatment?"

Mr O'Conner chimed in with a reply: "We find he responds well to them, sir."

"Young man, do you make a habit of responding to questions that were not addressed to you?"

"My apologies, sir."

Godalming looked as if he might be stifling a yawn. His hair, I noticed, was showing signs of receding: "It is occasionally necessary for us to give him a dunking, yes."

I first met the doctor two years previously, when he took over the running of the asylum from John Mitchell after an inmate hit the former over the head with a rock concealed in a sock. Aware he was well respected by the more Evangelical members of the Lunacy Commission, I distrusted him from the start. Although I had no reason to doubt he was a competent biologist and bookkeeper his skill as a Superintendent left much, in my view, to be desired.

A voice from down the corridor called for Mr O'Conner's assistance with another patient. After receiving a nod of approval from his superior the attendant hurried away. The inmate, I noticed, had shuffled into an upright position against the rubber cushioning and was regarding me as if he had something to say. Opening his mouth he strained his neck and let loose a series of guttural clucks. Outside, the peafowl were shrieking.

"What is it, Mr Arscott?"

"He cannot answer you," said Godalming. "He has no tongue."

"How did he lose it?"

"He bit it off, sad to say. When he was an adolescent."

Urgently struggling to form words the mute gulped and retched, threatening to vomit from the effort. Inside his mouth the short stump of what remained of his tongue was just visible.

"I suggest you have your man administer a sedative when he returns," I said.

"Naturally."

On our way to the lobby I was forced to listen to the Superintendent's tedious attempts at making conversation, describing the shortcomings of the building's plumbing system in near obsessive detail. Even he seemed bored by what he was saying. At the main door I interrupted him mid-sentence: "You will receive your report from the Commission sometime next week."

"Very well."

All the way down the long gravel path he insisted on accompanying me, now in silence, finally taking his leave at the grand lodge.

With mechanical formality he shook my hand: "Until we meet again."

He was already halfway back to the Gothic madhouse by the time my Brougham pulled away.

A Conversation with Doctor David Toynbee

DAVID was sitting in my drawing room, talking with his usual fervour but somehow ill at ease. Shifting his shoulders, he tapped at his pipe: "I don't suppose you witnessed the accident on Marylebone Road?"

"There was an accident?"

"It was in yesterday's paper. I wondered whether you might have passed it on your way to work on Monday morning."

"I saw nothing of it. What happened?"

"The horses of a travelling carriage took fright somehow and broke into a gallop. They mounted the pavement and turned the whole thing on its side. The passengers were largely unharmed, apparently, but a little girl was crushed under the wheels. Terribly sad. I'm surprised you didn't read about it."

I nodded and looked down at the surface of the table between us. Terribly sad news it was indeed, and it shocked me far more profoundly than I might have expected, so much so that when David continued to speak I barely listened.

Seeing I was distracted he broke off: "Feeling hippish again?"

"Sorry, David."

"Still having trouble with your sleep? You look dog-tired."

"It must be the hay fever. It goes to my chest and makes me drowsy. I had hoped moving away from the country would put an end to it."

"Perhaps the city itself is finally taking its toll. The dirt, the noise, the sheer vastness of it. The whole place is collapsing in on itself. There will be an exodus before too long, mark my words. It can wear a man down."

"No, no. I'm sure it's not that. Leaving Devon was absolutely the correct choice."

A combination of controversy and fortune had led me to make my move. I had for some months experienced a growing sense of dissatisfaction with the limitations of my office. Like many of my peers I found the remuneration I received in no way correlated with the strains of the work: the threat of abuse from the patients, the increasing influx of chronic cases, the morbid atmosphere. The metropolitan physician can expect to see his income increase as his reputation extends. The provincial asylum physician, regardless of experience or maturity, can enjoy scarcely more than a modest income, almost equivalent to even his youngest colleagues. It was necessary to speak out about this injustice and campaign for its rectification.

In addition to all this I felt compelled to express my

fierce distaste concerning recent appointments to the Lunacy Commission. Having been encouraged by the promotions of Samuel Greene and Henry Wilkes-eminent physicians deserving of such a tribute-my peers were forced to suffer the insult of finding ourselves governed by men utterly ignorant of life in an asylum. In a short space of time the likes of Winchester, Pugh and Drinkwater were nominated, regardless of their inexperience: Drinkwater in particular seeming to have only his Evangelism to thank for his appointment.

These ideas formed the basis of many of my contributions to both *The Mind* and that other esteemed publication *The Journal of Medical Science*, articles I considered to be rational and restrained which still managed to cause considerable outrage. The Earl of Shaftesbury-an Evangelist himself and clearly in sympathy with Drinkwater, Lutwidge and the likes-sent me an aggressively challenging letter. In the midst of such conflict I was unlikely to ever find myself promoted onto the Commission: an organisation in which I was, in any case, losing faith.

It was fortunate then, when faced with such dismal prospects and experiencing such an overwhelming disaffection for my profession-the exertion, the isolation, the salary-that the Lord Chancellor wrote me a letter offering me the prized appointment of Visitor in Lunacy.

Two positions had recently been vacated by Arthur Southey and Walter Bucknill, both men too old to continue carrying out their duties. Being a doctor of considerable ability and experience it was felt I would be an ideal replacement. I accepted the position with relief and gratitude. My income no less than tripled and London was my home within three months.

With the fire dying in the hearth David began to talk of his family, a sign the effects of the alcohol were beginning to take hold. When sober his conversation more-or-less stayed around subjects concerning our professions. Rocking his leg up and down he told me about his son's ambitions to become a lawyer and his daughter's burgeoning artistic flare: his whole house was becoming overrun with newly stitched crochets and patchwork quilts. Picking up his empty glass he turned it in his hand: "You never married, Richard."

Although I knew he meant well the words still sounded like an accusation.

"No."

"Through choice or circumstance?"

It was a topic we had never touched upon before. David happily spoke of his own domestic circumstances but never asked about my own. In raising the subject I felt he was breaking an unwritten rule. My answer was non-committal.

He asked if I had ever hoped to have a family of my own.

"I never gave the matter any consideration. Would you like me to pour you some more wine?"

"Come now," he persisted. "Surely it must have crossed your mind. It's natural for a man to want to extend his bloodline."

"I never expected to be married. Never strove for it."

"Did you not even want children?"

"I have had my work," I replied. "Besides, I was never much of an amorist. Wine?"

David frowned and accepted another refill.

Later in the entrance hall he paused under the frame of the open front door to straighten his coat. He intended to walk home rather than hail a cab, fancying himself a practised explorer of London's mazes and byways: "I am sorry if I made you uneasy earlier," he said with a slight slur which could only be detectable by someone who knew him well. "I was merely curious."

"Not at all. I wasn't uneasy in the least. It's been an extremely pleasant evening." The lock clicked as I shut the door.

Some hours later I woke into blackness. Recently my bad dreams had lost their shapelessness and taken on a powerful clarity. That night's had been the most vivid and frightening yet. I imagined myself strung up over the stairwell in my home, with my arms, legs and neck caught in loops of black hair the thickness of limbs. My hips were twisted and my head pulled painfully to the side. Hearing my housekeeper moving around on the ground floor I tried to call for help but found myself unable. With horror I realised my lips had been stitched together using a needle and thread. In a panic I struggled but to no avail, all the time knowing that even if I were to work my way free the resulting fall would break my spine. Trying again to shout I became aware of strange objects clustered around my teeth and gums which, using my tongue, I identified as insect larvae. Soon they would hatch and whatever creatures emerged would no doubt choke me. Farther down my throat, disturbed by my frantic movements, something awoke. It was small and rounded and encased in a hard shell. I froze, terrified of further aggravating this bodily invader. Only when it began to vibrate and produce a series of loud clicks did I realise it was an outsize Death Watch Beetle. It was at this point that the dream came to an end.

Lying awake I attempted to calm myself by imagining my uncle moving my twelve-year-old body into the correct posture for sleeping-pressing my palms flat on the mattress and sliding his hand under my back to check it was perfectly straight-but the awfulness of the dream refused to fade. It was no passing fright but one that deepened with time and communicated itself to the room, infecting its very walls.

As the first muted traces of morning light came through my window I became aware of minute movements on the ceiling above me. Dawn advanced and I saw it was a spider. Ensnared in its web was a tiny moth, around which the predator was weaving its silk threads. The process was enthralling. There was patience in the manner this work was completed, a fluid rhythm–limbs rotating and pulling–which I found hypnotic.

The day began, accompanied by the city's perpetual drone and clatter.

The Black Dog

I should have understood I was in danger when I noticed the man signalling me on the otherwise empty pavement ahead. Short, broad-shouldered and toothless he wore a shabby greatcoat over his slop and corduroy trousers tied at the ankles with string. I was walking home on Marylebone Road, where the accident David told me about had occurred a few days before. Since turning the corner I had been somewhat preoccupied, unable to stop myself picturing the little girl's broken body being pulled from beneath the carriage, a poor, fragile child lost in the spring of her hopes and beauty: a tragedy beyond comprehension. I searched my pocket for my handkerchief, suffering as usual with my hay fever.

Distracted by the sight of the shabby man waving his arms up and down in a way which struck me as ridiculous, I became aware of a tapping noise coming from somewhere behind me, increasing quickly in rapidity and volume. Before I could turn and investigate I was struck by a great weight that knocked me to the ground. Only by some force of instinct was I able to turn to my side to defend myself from the jaws of a ferocious black hound. Resisting all attempts to push it away the animal lurched insistently forward, its powerful jaws snapping mere inches from my face while I gripped its neck. Beneath its brittle pelt its taut muscles pulsed and strained. The beast was far stronger than I, and I knew that whatever force I could muster could never be enough. Hot foul breath mingled with my own, drool spattered my skin.

With relief I felt the monster's body being pulled away, its yellowish claws skittering backwards across the pavement. Three men had taken hold and were heaving it off, just at the moment the last of my strength was draining from my arms. If they had failed I am sure it would have torn a hole in my throat.

Slowly my surroundings came back into focus: black and white tiles around the doorway of a chemist, flowering weeds growing at the point where the building met the ground, a bright billboard advertising Allsop's Indian Pale Ale. My rescuers were holding the dog down and stamping at its ribs with their mud-encrusted boots, cursing in a European language I did not recognise. One of them, I now saw, was the shabby man in the greatcoat who had done his best to alert me. A cut-and-dry couple who had stopped to take in the spectacle moved on without offering me any assistance, along with a cab which had evidently slowed down for a better view. Struggling to my feet and retrieving my dropped handkerchief I saw that my right hand was bleeding. A heavy blow to the beast's exposed belly caused it to wail in a manner that sounded oddly human. With a wave of nausea I noticed it was sustaining a large, obscenely pink erection. That it might have been in such a state of arousal as it stood over me filled me with a raging disgust. I looked down at my trouser leg. The material was torn at the knee and marked by a shining web of semen. I fled the scene as quickly as I could, neglecting to thank my saviours, not because I was ungrateful but because I was worried I might vomit or faint. Crossing directly over to the park I hid amongst some bushes and wiped away as much of the stain as I could using a handful of leaves.

Ten minutes later I was entering my lodgings. I called for Miss Morley but received no reply. In the bathroom upstairs I ran my hand under some water then proceeded to the bedroom dresser, in which I kept a supply of lint and iodine. The puncture wound lay in the soft flesh between my thumb and forefinger. To stem the flow of blood while I prepared the dressing I held the wound to my mouth and sucked.

With a rap on the bedroom door Miss Morley finally announced herself. An unusually slender woman with striking silver hair, my housekeeper was in the habit of wringing her hands when she was in my company: "Have you been calling for me?"

"I have been calling for you since I entered the house."

She noted my dishevelled condition: my scuffed suit, my bleeding hand: "What happened?"

"I was attacked."

"Oh, Lord! By whom? One of your madmen?" Her Birmingham accent became more pronounced whenever she grew agitated.

"No. By a dog."

"Let me help you." Taking the bandages from me she set about dressing the wound.

"I was out on Marylebone Road. It was some kind of mongrel, I think. I swear it was intent on killing me. It was vicious. Vicious. I was lucky to escape with such minor injuries."

"You've ruined your trousers too, Doctor Renfield. What is that mark?"

Looking down I saw that the semen had left a pale stain. Appalled, I drew her attention back to my injury. "Miss Morley, please. You're binding that too tightly."

"Did it have an owner?"

"Pardon?"

"The dog. Did it belong to someone?"

"I don't know. I didn't see. I think it was a stray. It attacked me from behind, quite unprovoked. Three strong men were needed to drag the revolting thing from me. Vicious."

"Do you need to sit down? You've gone white as a

59

sheet."

"I'm perfectly well. I suffered a shock, that's all."

Again she glanced at my trousers: "I could repair those for you if you wanted."

"Yes. Thank you. I will leave them downstairs tomorrow."

She continued her work in silent concentration. When she tied the final knot she looked as if she might be about to ask me something.

"What is it?"

"Nothing, really. Nothing important. I meant to ask if everything had been well with you last night."

"In what sense?"

"Last night, after you retired."

"I was perfectly fine. Why do you ask?"

"I fancied I could hear your voice. I thought you had taken in another visitor after Doctor Toynbee left. Perhaps the elderly gentleman who was waiting on the street outside."

"What gentleman?"

"Very tall, thin, expensively dressed. I saw him outside the kitchen window. I presumed you knew him."

"I'm sorry. I don't know who you mean."

"I was sure I heard you talking to someone. You sounded upset."

"I cannot say what you heard, Miss Morley, but I can

assure you the voices did not originate from my room. I was sound asleep before eleven thirty, much as usual, and heard nothing."

"I thought it best to make sure."

"Someone must have been talking on the square. It is normal to hear activity there after dark: people coming home from the theatre, that kind of thing. I have been woken by it myself on occasion."

"Well, I thought it best. Never mind."

"Or perhaps you were dreaming. This is equally possible. Now, please bring me a pot of green tea. I have a good deal of work I intend to complete tonight and I have lost enough time already."

"Certainly, Doctor Renfield. If you want those trousers mending remember to leave them out for me."

After she had brought up my drink and returned to the ground floor I changed my clothes-careful to keep from touching what was left of the revolting stain-and took them out to soak. Returning to my room I felt compelled to sit on the edge of the bed. My heart was racing. Putting my hands to my face I closed my eyes, feeling the bandage press against my cheek. Before long the strong, chestnut-like aroma of the green tea penetrated the gaps between my fingers. Finding it suddenly repellent I carried the pot to the bathroom where my trousers lay submerged and poured the steaming liquid down the sink.

Flying Ants

I had taken a bench on the Broad Walk in Regent's Park, opposite the fountains where I first set eyes on the lady with the runaway parasol. It was early in the day—the park gates had only recently been unlocked—and the air was cool and still. By my side the flowerbeds were dense with irises.

We had seen each other on numerous occasions since the day we first met, acknowledging one another with a simple nod of the head or a smile, then later with a familiar 'good morning'. Her cordiality helped convince me that my attempt to rescue her parasol had been welcome, and my blunderous balancing act had not made me appear too foolish.

These encounters caused me to ponder the nature of her relationship with the child in the pram. At first I naturally assumed she was its mother but the more I thought about it the more convinced I became she must be its nanny. If she wore a wedding band, for example, I had failed to notice it. In order to resolve the mystery I determined to check her ring finger next time we met.

A sparrow settled amongst the flowers. Keeping quite still I watched it pecking through the soil, skipping and fluttering about. My hand throbbed. Despite my regular attentions the wound refused to heal. It would soon be necessary to visit the chemist to replenish my supply of lint.

Listening to the bees murmur drowsily between the blooms my mind began to wander, as it was recently prone to do. The sounds and smells of spring had once again brought forth memories of my childhood trips to the old bridge.

Although we didn't know it at the time it was our final summer together. I had changed a good deal since the year before, the natural ageing process and my commitment to out-of-door sports having made me physically robust, expanding my chest and giving me powerful, muscular limbs. People frequently mistook me to be much older than I actually was: I was easily the tallest boy in my school. Greeting me at the end of my driveway Oscar patted my back and remarked that living with Uncle Patrick was clearly having a positive influence on me. If Magdalene noticed my improved physique she made no comment, merely smiling quietly from her seat.

Patrick Renfield's enthusiasm for athletic pursuits was well known around the county, even after his sudden decline in health. Before his wife's death he had been a champion of the Volunteer movement, putting his every effort into promoting public sports with such enthusiasm his name was even painted above the door of the local drill-shed. It was his firm belief that a game of football or cricket was conducive not only to physical well-being but also moral health. A man's body was a gift from God, intended to be trained to its highest ability, for use as tool in the protection of the weak and the advance of religious causes.

The rapidity with which he passed into the state of a chronic invalid dismayed everyone who witnessed it. I had been under his care for a mere two months when a night spent under the stars during a weekend walking expedition triggered a near fatal attack of rheumatic fever from which he was never to recover. Confined to his home he found himself no longer able to set an example to Yorkshire's sporting youth, reduced to wondering the corridors of his home in his dressing gown and cane, his body withering and his vitality lost. It was fortunate that I arrived in his life in time to provide a focus for his passions, giving him someone to coach and encourage. I believe we both benefited from the relationship, even if I occasionally felt he was driving me too fiercely.

Although the activity had begun to feel childish, Magdalene and I still checked off the journey's familiar landmarks as they passed by: the valley, the post box, the row of shops. That morning the whitewashed cottages reflected the dazzling and all-pervading sunlight so vividly it was necessary to squint to look at them. It was I who first noticed the flying ants, when one flew through the gap in the window and landed on my shirt cuff. I held it up to my face to examine it more closely. It moved around on the landscape of white cotton, testing the surface with its tiny legs. That ants even possessed wings was a revelation to me.

Oscar explained, in that distracted way of his, tugging his beard as if his mind was on higher things: "Some are winged, most are not. The winged ants remain inside the parent colony for almost all of their lives, which is why they're not a familiar sight."

Now we had spotted one flying ant we saw them everywhere, tiny specks darting through the summer air, swarming at intervals along the road. Considering myself an expert in matters entomological, it was humiliating to have this crucial gap in my knowledge exposed. My companions, I decided, must think me laughably ignorant. I flicked our uninvited passenger back out of the window.

Magdalene asked what they were doing: why had they left the protection of their colonies. Her accent had altered slightly since the previous year—a result of her spending the spring in the Scottish Highlands—and her voice sounded loud in the confines of the carriage.

"In order to mate," said Oscar.

Instantly my face flushed. It was embarrassing to hear such indelicate matters discussed openly.

"How do they know to launch all at once? It's like magic."

"I'm sorry to admit I have no idea. Something to do with weather conditions, perhaps. After all, they couldn't very well fly about in the rain, could they? I'll endeavour to find out and let you know. Even better: why don't you find out and tell me?"

Soon we had disembarked and were strolling across the grassy field towards the bridge, the occasional ant flying past us or landing on our clothes. The weather was perfect, the sky was bright and cloudless and the air agreeably fresh. With a flourish Oscar unfurled his woollen blanket.

A delightful afternoon passed, taken up with us throwing a ball around and exploring the outer reaches of the field. Sitting with his legs crossed Magdalene's father read to us from Coleridge's *To the River Otter*. Finally dusk fell and the sky turned orange and purple then dark blue. Oscar, packing up the remains of the picnic ready for our departure, explained that on such nights, when the moon was shining with particular intensity, there was an observable increase in spiritual activity: hysterics became agitated, dreams became more vivid, those with a tendency towards nervousness found themselves upset and confused.

"Its influence on living things should not be underestimated. Did you know that many plants and vegetables grow more quickly when the moon is at its fullest? Cucumbers, leeks, radishes: they all seem to draw sustenance from the rays. Not onions, though. I don't know why."

As I stood admiring the bright white disc I was surprised by a black object flashing by at great speed some twenty yards away. I insisted my companions stop loading the hamper so they could watch. Another shape darted in the opposite direction, cutting a swift arc over the bridge.

"Bats," exclaimed Oscar. "They must be picking off the last of the ants."

It was impossible to say how many there were in total: they were too fast to count. All we could do, we agreed, was select a spot on which to focus our gaze and wait for them to flit by. At times it seemed as if many dozens were criss-crossing the sky above us, their wings beating so fast they were almost invisible.

Entranced by this display I was startled to feel Magdalene's hand searching for my own. She was close by my side while her father stood looking away from us on the blanket with his head raised and his hands on his hips. Eagerly I reached out and took hold of it, still looking at the sky despite my immediate loss of interest in the bat's evening feast. Her palm felt soft against my own. After few moments standing like this she leant over, placed her thumb on my chin and kissed my lips, clumsily and quickly so that our teeth knocked together. Resuming her previous position she turned her face upwards as if nothing had happened. Keen to communicate my lack of objection I gave her hand a squeeze.

When she was suitably confident her father was still transfixed by the bats she took the opportunity to turn around and kiss me again, with tenderness this time and risking a few seconds more. I remember thinking her lips were colder than I imagined lips would be and the breath from her nostrils felt strange on my skin.

"Remarkable, no?" said Oscar, looking over his shoulder. Our hands unlocked and Magdalene jumped back, but it was too late. We had been caught.

Making no remark he turned away. A period of strained silence followed as we all watched the bats, then: "Let's pack the rest of this up and get back to the coach, shall we? We don't want to worry your uncle."

The sparrow launched and suddenly I was back in Regent's Park. Half a worm hung from the tiny bird's beak. The other half remained poking up from the soil. Mist from the distant fountains drifted like a procession of phantoms across the promenade. There was still no sign of the nanny.

The park was beginning to fill up, people taking morning strolls or pacing purposefully to work. The previous evening it occurred to me that, now I had exchanged so many greetings with my new acquaintance, failing to strike up a proper conversation might be considered rude. It was for this reason I had arrived in the park so much earlier than usual and taken up my spot on the bench. If she happened to pass my way I would ask how she was and perhaps remark on the prettiness of the baby. Any exchange we shared would not need to be rushed or cut short. Consulting my pocket watch I resolved to stay where I was until it became absolutely necessary for me to leave to catch my train.

Incident of the Letter

THAT night my sleep was once more disturbed, this time not by night terrors or strange hallucinations but by a dream so brightly lit and lifelike I became bewildered, unsure whether I was sleeping or awake.

I imagined myself strolling through the grounds of Devon County Asylum, following the fence along the edge of the neighbouring farmer's field. From the direction of the orchard an indistinct figure approached, pushing a pram through the mud with remarkable ease. As she drew closer I recognised her as the young woman from the park. That she might be here—in a different time and a different place—did not strike me as in any way odd. Once we were close to speak enough she stopped and enquired after my health, suggesting we might stroll together for a while.

Some way down the track she spotted an injured hare by the foot of a wooden stile, twitching strangely and not quite dead. She asked if I thought there was any way we could help.

"No," I said. "It's time in this world is over."

"So sad."

I nodded and we carried on. Shortly we found ourselves approaching the old bridge over the River Esk in

Yorkshire. It being a hot day I suggested we take a paddle to cool ourselves off. As we climbed down to the water's edge and removed our footwear I asked her name: "I can't imagine why I never thought to find it out before."

"How strange! Elise. My name is Elise."

"It suits you."

We waded in until the cold water was around our knees. A light breeze shook the trees on the far bank and blossoms spun through the summer air.

"It's been so many years since I was last here," I said. "I used to come here all the time. I can't think why I stopped. It hasn't changed at all."

The moment I finished speaking a stunning phosphorescence ignited over the water. Standing in awed silence we watched it slowly drift by. Then suddenly light was building all around us, playing around our bodies and above our heads. Lifting our arms we laughed as it looped and swirled over and under our limbs. Countless shimmering minnows gathered and danced at our feet. Mingling and becoming one with the drifting blossoms the luminescence reflected from the river so dazzlingly I was forced to shut my eyes....

When I woke it was disorienting find myself back in my dreary London bedroom. Taking the dream to be a blessing and a sign I tried to keep it in my mind so I could remember it forever, but by the time I had dressed for work some of the smaller details were already starting to fade. I was sure someone else had been with us, for example, perhaps in the trees beyond the far bank, but I could not remember who.

Miss Morley was waiting for me in the hallway, absent-mindedly wringing her hands: "Is your injury healing, Doctor Renfield?"

I had once again applied fresh bandages but saw no sign of improvement: "It's coming along very well, thank you. Is there something you wanted?"

She jolted, as if emerging from a trance: "Oh, yes. Yes: a letter for you."

Thanking her I left, waiting until I was on the train before I unsealed the registered envelope. It was from Mrs Utterson.

DEAR DR RENFIELD: Will I never be free from adversity? We have suffered yet another disaster. Two weeks ago my husband made an attempt on his own life. Whether this was the result of his mental disorder or pure despair I cannot tell. He has now returned from the hospital and rests in his room with a member of staff permanently at his door.

I hope you will find it in your heart to see us, if you can. My family labours under a blackness of distress and at present there is scarcely a gleam of light to guide me. Serve me, Dr Renfield, and save.

Indigestion

MRS Utterson once more received me in the drawing room of her villa. Through the bay widow fell a cold and muted light. The atmosphere was comfort-less and dismal.

"What happened to your hand, Doctor Renfield?"

"I had an accident with the window pane in my study. It was nothing; a foolish thing."

"Is the cut deep?"

"Hardly a graze."

Under the table the grey cat dozed, its delicate ribcage rising and falling. The giant rubber plant, I noticed, had been moved from where it previously stood and now occupied the shadowy opposite corner of the room where it was failing to flourish, its leaves covered with a thick layer of household dust. The Chesterfield had shifted too so that it faced towards the wall. Dark shadows troubled Mrs Utterson's her eyes and her hands trembled gently, constantly.

"I am sorry you had to make the journey from Marylebone again so soon."

"Don't let it concern you. I'm happy to help."

Around her neck she wore a plaid band that seemed to me to be too tight. My instinct was to slip my finger beneath the material and hook it away but I resisted. Above the fireplace the painting of the River Esk remained, its colours diminished in the gloom but still capable of making a powerful claim on my attention.

"My husband is sleeping," she told me.

Tearing my gaze away I regarded her: "Yes?"

"We took his key away, as you recommended," she said, "although he still insists on keeping his door closed." Woken by our voices, the cat stirred and arched its back. "I cannot sleep for fear of what further harm he might cause himself. Sometimes I think the torment is greater than I can bear. If sorrow could kill me I ought to have died before this." Attempting to make myself less uncomfortable I uncrossed my legs. My feet felt heavy and my thighs ached. Every move I made felt grossly exaggerated. "I suppose I should tell you the nature of the horror that befell us."

"May I see the patient?"

Startled by the sharpness of my interruption she hesitated: "Of course. I will accompany you. I must warn you I cannot be sure how he will react. His behaviour towards the servants has been unusually hostile."

"In what way? Has he been violent?"

"No, never. The only violence committed has been on his own person. He has been accusing the staff of stealing from him. He says they break in while he sleeps and

75

remove his things. When he speaks of it he becomes extremely upset. I cannot stand to see it, Doctor."

Readjusting its position, the cat-who had been pawing lazily at my shoe-prepared to jump onto my lap. Misjudging the distance it slipped and fell to the floor. For the first time I saw its corneas were misty white and a sticky residue lined its lower lids.

"What is wrong with your pet?"

"She is going blind. She will have lost her sight completely before the summer is over."

"A pity."

After making a second failed attempt the poor creature gave up and trotted towards the door. Anxiety beamed from Mrs Utterson's face: "I have visions, Doctor Renfield."

I did not speak.

"I see my husband strung up by ropes threaded through a series of hooks on the ceiling. They bind his torso and limbs so he struggles but cannot escape. Along the wall is a row of chairs, occupied by gentlemen in dark suits and black gloves. They watch him without emotion and make no attempt to help." Leaning forward she took hold of my knee. "But I do not think they are visions, Doctor Renfield. I think they are real."

Her lips were cracked and her skin was flaking and dry. Gripped by a sudden cold revulsion I was compelled to push her hand away and get to my feet.

"Let's go."

On the first floor we passed the room from where I heard the mysterious clicking on my previous visit. The door was fully open and as I went by I saw it had been almost entirely emptied of furniture except for an upturned chair and gate-leg table covered by a square of black material. Although my view was obscured I felt certain someone lurked within.

Mrs Utterson led me on to the third floor, where the scent of the flowers had been all but overpowered by the repugnant smell of stale tobacco. The bouquets had wilted and fallen petals lay on the carpet. Reaching the final step she turned suddenly, blocking my ascent and forcing me to lean back, holding on to the banister with one hand for support. I wondered if I should mention I was feeling unwell.

"It was I who discovered him," she said.

"I do not want to know."

"But you must hear it."

"Please, no."

"He was lying on the floor beside his writing desk, his head between the legs of his chair. There were deep bite marks running up both of his arms and his left wrist was missing a piece of flesh. Of course, he had lost a good deal of blood. All the books had been thrown from the shelves and scattered around the floor. I did my best to bind the wounds while the housemaid sent for the private attendant. It was he who extracted the missing piece of flesh from the back of my husband's throat."

She was breathing heavily. With nothing more to say we stood mutely at the top of the stairs. My vision became indistinct. For a moment I believed there was nothing behind me: no steps, no walls. Only blackness and an abyssal drop.

Clawing at my shoulders she pressed her lips forcefully against my own. I stumbled backwards but managed to save myself. Breath hissed from her nose in short bursts. Her eyes fluttered wildly beneath their lids while mine remained open. Blood rushed in my ears and the walls seemed to shake and roar, as if the bricks might crumble and collapse. Unbuckling my belt with my uninjured hand I tugged my trousers down and pushed her to the floor as she lifted her dress. I was overwhelmed by noise. Mr Utterson's door loomed behind me, so strongly I believed I could feel the solid wood pressing down against my back. There on the carpet we wrestled with each other, lost in a bewildered state of carnality and violence. Everything was shrouded in white.

In an instant, like a finger snap, my full cognisance returned and with extreme clarity I could see Mrs Utterson's shoulder moving beneath me. Her body was twisted, her hands clasping my head and her white-grey thighs tight around my waist, jerking and twitching, while she emitted a series of strangled gasps. My hips thrust against hers, knocking her lower back against the hard lip of the stair. I ejaculated inside her despite my deep revulsion.

Depleted, we lay together, my full heft rested on her body and her arms spread across the floor. Silence grew around the two of us. Finally pushing myself away a sharp pain shot from my wound. Fumbling, I struggled to pull my trousers up, mortified to be exposing myself. She was spent and staring blankly at the ceiling, apparently oblivious to me. I turned and made my way carefully down to the ground floor, sliding my hand along the banister for support.

After collecting my bag from the hallway I walked to the station and took the train to Marylebone. From here, rather than return home, I began to walk east, towards Bloomsbury and Clerkenwell, entering parts of London which, although I may have recognised them in the daytime, seemed foreign to me now.

Much later I came across a part of the nocturnal city where there was nothing to be seen but lamps. Every step was lighted as if for a procession but all was empty. A thick dark fog slept above the buildings. At street level there seemed to be an excess of air.

Far ahead I caught sight of two women strolling arm in arm along the pavement. Because of their relaxed pace I was able to catch up without any effort, eventually drawing level on the opposite side of the road. As they crossed between the flickering pools of light, they seemed unaware they were being watched. At this proximity I had no difficulty in recognising one of them as the young woman from Regent's Park.

The Familiar

I slowed down and waited for the distance between us to increase, fixing my gaze on the back of the nanny's head: her smooth neckline and her unblemished white skin. After crossing to her side of the roadway, treading as lightly as I could, I concealed myself in a butcher shop's doorway. Resting my hand on the blistered architrave I discovered a crude carving, a blasphemous word. The shifting fog dropped, weighty in the night sky.

Only once the women had turned the corner did I emerge from my hiding place and make after them. Finding my business bag cumbersome I dropped it behind a garden fence with the intention of collecting it later, then stopped to peer around the side of the wall just in time to see them disappearing down another street. Somewhere in the distance a dog dispatched a single bark like a pistol shot. Through this new and sparsely lit thoroughfare I followed, sidestepping into doorways and alcoves whenever I feared I might be detected.

I cannot say for how long I pursued them, or how far. I only wished to reassure myself that all was well with Elise and no personal misfortune had prevented her from taking her morning walks. I was also intrigued by the presence of the second woman. Who could she be? The two of them were clearly at ease with each other, strolling arm in arm and quietly chatting. Was she Elise's friend? Her sister?

Eventually we came upon a procession of houses overlooking a stretch of undeveloped land. The night air was crisp and tasted something like metal. I was unusually conscious of my breathing, needing to concentrate to keep it regular. Small sounds carried far. Preceded by her footfalls a bony-faced girl of eight or nine years emerged from the darkness, sprinting headlong and as fast as she was able. A few moments later she was followed by a big-bellied man with a thick beard. Elise's companion—a slender woman with pearl-white skin and yellow hair—looked inquisitively over her shoulder towards them, adjusting her gloves. The little girl bolted past me and away down an alleyway, her expression a mixture of determination and terror. Red faced and panting, her pursuer paused in the middle of the road and rested his hands on his knees before hopelessly lumbering off again. With them both out of sight, the yellow haired woman glanced suspiciously in my direction. I had been spotted.

There being nowhere to hide I had little choice but to keep walking as if nothing had happened. Following in the steps of the bearded man down the alley would have meant turning on my heels, an act that could only make me appear even more sinister, something I dearly wished to avoid if Elise had already recognised me from the park. How could I explain myself? I reduced my speed but seemed unable to extend the gap. Stopping briefly I made a show of consulting my pocket watch, lowering my head and hoping the night would obscure my features.

When I looked up again the women had vanished. Caught in a sudden panic I ran forward, struck by the realisation I might never cross paths with the young nanny again and my opportunity to spark a relationship with her would be missed forever. To my relief I saw they had turned another corner and were now opening a wrought iron gate towards the end of a row of Georgian terraces.

"Elise!" I yelled. "Elise!"

Either oblivious or indifferent to me they climbed the steps to an opening red door, their faces caught in the light from the hallway within. A gentleman reached out and took Elise's hand.

Once they were inside I strode down the street and hid myself in a narrow space between two adjacent buildings, from where I could see the plain black door. Faint light was visible behind the curtained windows across the thoroughfare. The iron gate had been closed.

It was in this alleyway that I lived for the coming days.

A Vigil

WHEN I woke it appeared to be morning. The fog had thinned and one or two factory workers were moving about. I had been sleeping on my feet-something to which I had quickly grown accustomed-my shoulder propped against the alley wall and brick dust on my disarranged coat. Attempting to straighten myself I was forced to sit on the ground, having lost strength in my legs. With my uninjured hand I wiped the dust away and rested my head on the loose water pipe running down the side of the building. It was early enough for most people to still be in bed.

I was angry I had allowed myself to drift into unconsciousness for what must have been at least an hour. It had been my wish to dispense with sleep altogether but my body betrayed me and made it impossible. The best I could do was nap as sparingly and as lightly as possible. Because of my night terrors I had been living on precious little rest for months now, so I felt confident I could survive on four hours a day. I divided my sleep into segments, as best I could. Twenty minutes every two hours. This duration seemed ideal, long enough to provide quietus but too short for anything but the shallowest slumber. It was my hope that any significant noises–the red door opening, the sound of Elise's voice–would pull me back into wakefulness. Was it possible the young nanny had left the house while I was insensible? An undisciplined moment may have caused me to squander my last chance to see her. My stomach turning at this notion I pulled myself to my feet, striking a pose that suggested alertness in the hope of encouraging it. I could not allow myself to be so reckless.

It is impossible to give an accurate account of my extended stay in the alleyway. Whether I was there for a week, or two weeks, or simply a matter of days, I cannot say. No memory of this period is certain and my recollection has no sequence, as if it all happened at once. Despite the inhospitable conditions it was not an entirely unhappy time. I found some pleasure in the protracted nature of the task, the feat of endurance. I was unburdened by society, my only concern being the continuation of the watch. I existed in a strange place, beyond ordinary human concerns, where the only markers were the occasional need to eat, sleep and excrete.

For much of the time I gave no thought to food. I even believed I could survive without it, finding my nourishment from sunlight alone. Sometimes, however, I became so gripped by hunger my whole body shook. I saw everything in double, fluctuating colours floated before my

85

eyes and a terrifying pain tore through my belly. I retched but was unable to vomit, convinced I was dying. These pangs, though, never failed to pass and my vigilance returned.

I did not go completely without sustenance. The small amount of money I had on my person was enough to purchase a pot of jam and two loaves of bread on my first morning, from a small grocer at the end of the road. Having no knife to use I tore pieces off the loaves and spread the jam using the fingers of my good hand. The first portions were eaten quickly but later I learnt to ration them, consuming only a bite or two at a time. Once the bread had been finished I ate the jam on its own, scooping it from the bottom of the jar and getting blackberry seeds lodged uncomfortably beneath my fingernails. My body stopped producing stools. I urinated thickly and odorously behind the pipe.

All this time I thought about the man who had answered the door to the two women. Even though I had not seen his face I fancied I could picture it, and I hated it, hated him. Doubtless he would have no appreciation of how fortunate he was to be in his position, in the company of a person as special as Elise. I wondered if, perhaps, he should be reminded of this somehow, taught a lesson.

At night, when the street was empty, I was confident enough to stand at the alley's entrance. In hours of concourse I stepped into the shadows. Blocking the pedestrians from my consciousness I focussed only on the door.

I perceived my surroundings with greater acuity than I ever believed might be possible. The small world I had created rushed in on me with luminous clarity: the fantastic and multitudinous hues of the fog and the shafts of light which glanced through it; the tiniest details of the red bricks. It was as if my eyes had never fully opened before. A veil had been lifted.

Unable to clean the dressing around my hand it inevitably caused an infection. The wound prickled and suppurated. Ants crawled about the lint. Picking them off I swallowed them for nourishment.

When it rained I sat on the ground and huddled behind the loose pipe, my frock coat pulled over my head…

… A drainage grill. The hard ground.

At the far end of the passage, a black dog with its tail docked, watching me...

Sunshine reflecting brilliantly from puddles...

...I have suffered enough. No more now.

The sound of a tongue clucking or the snapping of fingers. I am not alone. Someone takes me in their arms. I rest my weight against the old man, rubbing my cheek against his silk coat. His smell is familiar, like woodland undergrowth after a storm.

Long fingernails trace a line across my forehead and down my cheek. Gently, he parts my lips.

Black silk, wet soil, the rich odour of his breath.

PART TWO

"Place your hands on your chest," says the German beneath the black sheet. "Cross them over."

Emerging from behind the camera he takes my wrists and crosses them for me. He is a heavy-bodied man in a brightly coloured waistcoat, someone I recognise from the distant past, with a greying swallow-tailed beard.

"Palms down."

Distracted, I fail to respond.

"Palms down," he says again.

Over my shoulder is a square mirror angled to display my profile. Breaking my pose once more I turn to study my new face. It is similar to my old face but shrunken and wrinkled, its fallen cheekbones coloured by burst capillaries. My hair is spiky and uneven, having been carelessly shaved and allowed to grow back. Studying its silver flecks I move my head slowly from side to side.

"Please try to remain stationary."

This new face reminds me of my uncle. I had never seen the resemblance before but now I am older I can detect similarities in our bone structure, in the shape of my head, as if he is growing within me, replacing me by stealth, emerging from under my skin.

In a final attempt to regain my attention the German gives a single, sharp clap of his hands. I fire him a stern look but already he has disappeared beneath the sheet. Electricity shoots through the copper conductors which touch against my cheeks and my muscles spasm, forcing me into a clownish grin. Although I am expecting the blinding flash I am startled by its brightness and react by throwing my arm across my eyes, knocking the conductors out of position. Once the photograph has been taken I relax but find I prefer to keep my arm where it is, comforted by the sensation of being removed from the world.

The German sighs resignedly: "Take him away."

Sensing the duty attendant is drawing near I get to my feet and allow him to take me by the elbow. A metallic odour invades the air: the magnesium from the flash. Slowly I am directed out of the studio and on to the tiled floor of the corridor. My fellow inmates shuffle by, some chattering or moaning, others silent. Past the bath-house I am led, where I can hear a shower being administered, towards the tailor's shop and cook's store and the infirmary. Keeping my eyes closed I bury my nose in the crook of my arm and breathe in the soapy smell of the material. My guide warns me when we are about to climb the echoing stairwell to the second floor. On reaching the top I open one eye and take a peek: ahead of me is a long, wide passage with a polished wooden floor, a row of closed doors fitted with observation hatches, and the back of my attendant's peaked hat.

Only when I am alone inside my private room do I feel safe enough to take down my arm. Someone has moved my chair. Picking it up by the backrest I put it down in its proper spot: five feet from the side walls, six from the front and rear: the position I find most conducive to serious thought. I am well provided for here: I have a bedside table, a shelf full of books, a comfortable bed and a wardrobe containing three waistcoats, three pairs of drawers, three undervests, four shirts, four collars and four pocket handkerchiefs.

After slipping into a period of entrancement I am woken by the sound of the escape sirens being tested, blaring outwards from our position on the hill top and frightening the birds into silence. I uncross my legs and stand, my face still tingling slightly from the electric shocks. Browsing through my books I find nothing to engage me.

The observation hatch in the door snaps open and shut and Hardy backs his way in, carrying a tray.

"Food," he says. A pocket watch chain dangles loosely from the waistcoat of his cheaply cut uniform. Brusquely handing me my meal he casts me his usual bug-eyed look of undisguised contempt. His face is red and his neck is too wide for his head.

"Tell me again: why do you get to eat in your room when nearly everyone else has to go to the dining room? Too good to brush shoulders with the riff raff?"

I look down at my meal: "You've spilt it."

On the plate a few boiled potatoes and carrots sit next to a fatty cut of beef. Some of the gravy has slopped over the lip and pooled around edges. My mug of tea is monogrammed with the name of the institution: Carfax Criminal Lunatic Asylum.

"So it has," he says, and walks away.

In the moment before he closes the door behind him I speak again: "Ape."

He turns back and makes a show of casually resting against the frame, his thumb slotted into his belt buckle and his hips sloping in a way which makes him look unintentionally womanly: "What was that?"

Looking him in the face I repeat the word, enunciating carefully to ensure he understands: "Ape."

A few swift paces and he smacks the tray's underside, propelling my meal into the air. Gravy splashes on my shirt and the plate clatters across the floorboards: "Sorry, I didn't quite hear you. What did you say?"

He is willing me to defend myself, to provide an excuse to dish out a hiding. Instead I offer him a broad smile.

"Fucking idiot," he says.

Once the door has closed I kneel down and set about scooping up a few handfuls of the brown liquid, along with the beef. When I have collected a sufficient amount I leave the rest of the gravy and the potatoes—one of which has rolled under the bed-and take the tray to the window. The wooden shutter is open and the sash is raised. I stop for a moment to consider the view. Aside from a regularly spaced line of trees running along the left side of the distant horizon the landscape is featureless: no farmhouses, no hedgerows, no roads, and no buildings. Only a dun sky and drizzle. No signs of human activity at all.

Taking a dollop of sauce I slap it down and smear it across the sill, covering the dried remains of my previous offering. On top of this goes the slice of fatty meat. Gravy drips thinly down the wall.

*

The observation hatch snaps open, closes again. I am lying fully clothed on my bed, shoes and all. A youthful, sandy haired gentleman puts his head around the door, peering over gold rimmed spectacles with intensely blue eyes: "May I?"

"What a fatuous question."

Stepping forward he reveals himself to be tall and

richly attired, dressed in the finest of broadcloth with a broad-folded tie of a design I fancy I recognise.

"Thank you," says the stranger to the attendant in the corridor. "There is no reason for you to accompany me farther." He extends his hand to me: "Doctor Seward."

It has been so long since anyone has introduced themselves in this way I am unsure how to respond and remain where I am.

He continues: "I am the new Superintendent. I will be overseeing your treatment from now on."

"What happened to Carey?"

"Doctor Carey has taken a post elsewhere." He gestures to my chair. "Do you mind if I sit?"

Placing himself in the centre of the room he straightens his trousers, a gesture both energetic and precise.

"I have been looking through your records. Your case intrigues me."

"Is that so?"

I swing my legs over the edge of the mattress and face my visitor. His skin is smooth and his countenance boyish, making it difficult to guess his age, although a Superintendent must at the very least be in his third decade.

"My predecessor was under the impression you are harbouring a great secret. It was his opinion that you have fixed on some mysterious plan that you are determinedly following, although he could only speculate on what it might be. He left me reams of notes on the topic, folders full of them."

I am beginning to think I may have underestimated this young man at first sight. The point he makes strikes me as worth pondering. Am I busy working towards some goal, the nature of which is a mystery even to me? It is a riveting concept and one which stimulates my scientific mind.

"Is there something in this claim, do you think?" the doctor continues.

I deliberate over my reply: "Perhaps."

"Tell me, do you know why you are here?"

"I have my suspicions."

"What have you been told? Did Doctor Carey address the issue?"

"I'm here for my own safety; for the safety of others. It all depends on to whom I am speaking when I ask the question."

"What do can remember of the events which brought you to this place?"

"I remember being shackled in a landau with a shivering young man who reeked of mothballs. I remember winding country roads, tall hedges and livestock. I remember a steep hill, and being taken through two gates, one green and one black. I remember guards and heavily barred windows."

"Very good, but you misunderstand me. What do you recall of the circumstances which led to your incarceration?"

I shake my head.

"You attacked someone in the street, yes? Did you know that?"

"That is what I have been told."

"The gentleman in question was passing through his garden gate when you ran across the road and struck him over the head with a length of pipe. You had been missing from your home for a number of days and had, it appears, been hiding in an alleyway. Once he fell to the ground you continued to beat him until three bystanders intervened and wrestled you away. They are convinced you would have killed him otherwise. Does any of this make sense to you?"

"Of course it makes sense to me. Whether I accept it as the truth is another matter."

"Your victim is yet to recover and is completely unable to speak. What do you think about that? It appears your actions were unprovoked. Had the jury not considered you to be of unsound mind you would have undoubtedly been found guilty of attempted murder. As it is, you are detained in Carfax until Her Majesty's pleasure be known. How does that make you feel?"

"That the truth must be uncovered."

Sitting back in the chair Seward notices my open window: "There are flies on your sill."

Three bluebottles skitter on the rotting meat, great big fat ones with steel and sapphire on their wings. I raise my hand, gesturing for the doctor to remain perfectly still. Taking care to keep from making any sudden movements I reach over to my bedside table and collect the monogrammed tea cup that came with my meal. Gradually I stand and creep towards my prize before bringing to container down in one fluid movement. Two of the flies escape but one remains.

Seward has been quietly observing: "This is a victory for you?"

I tip the cup and take the tiny creature in my fist: "Clearly you underestimate the skill required to catch a fly."

"Not in the least. It is an impressive feat. Are you going to let it go now?"

I am about to reply when I am once again distracted by my visitor's broad-folded tie. It is white, speckled with lilac, and seems entirely familiar. Suddenly I am struck by the queasy notion that it used to belong to me. The thought arrives with a tightening in my chest and frightening pain, like a hot needle thrust into my right temple. A vision comes, of my younger self checking my appearance in the mirror which hung in the entrance hall of my Marylebone lodgings, the speckled tie hanging around my neck.

I press my fist to my head, feeling the fly struggling against my palm.

"Are you unwell, Renfield?"

There is only one explanation: I am Doctor Seward; Doctor Seward is me. One soul rent in two.

"Renfield?"

On the heels of the intensifying pain comes a blinding light, rushing in around me like a wave. Acrid bile rises in my throat and my legs collapse beneath me.

"Hardy!" Seward calls for assistance, urgently but without alarm. "Hardy! Come here, would you?"

*

The cold wakes me. I am face down on the bed and naked, unable to recall whether I undressed myself. Afraid I might suffer another influx of light I keep my eyes tightly shut.

Time passes and eventually I put my hand to my face and risk looking through my fingers. It is night and the shutters are closed. Lying perfectly still I watch my room take form as my eyes grow accustomed to the dark: the edge of the mattress, the chair, the bookshelf on the far wall.

Every attack is the same: a sudden and alarming pain in

my right temple, followed by an extreme peripheral white light that quickly spreads and consumes my entire field of vision. The experience is so excruciating I become bewildered and prone to entertaining irrational thoughts. Breathing here steadily in the cool dark, I understand perfectly well that Seward and I do not share a soul. The whole idea seems preposterous. But it can be hard to remain sensible when one is in agony. Finally I take my hand down from my eyes.

Outside, my guards are changing shifts. During the day my room is left unlocked and I am allowed to wander about as I wish, overseen by the attendant who sits beside the gas-jet at the end of the corridor. As the sun sets the door is locked and guarded by unseen night watchers. Staring down at the hair on my chest I listen to them talk.

"He died a week ago. Went to bed feeling faint one night and never woke up. His wife found him beside her in the morning, stone cold."

"What are they saying it was?"

"No-one knows. It was right out of the blue. My wife's convinced a plague's on the way."

"Mine too, and my kids. Our neighbour fell ill and the whole household went into a panic. I couldn't make them see sense. I said to them: what's the point in getting into a flap? There's nothing much we could do about it even if it were true."

They exchange good-nights and one of them leaves to go home, his footsteps trailing away down the corridor. The remaining watcher lights his pipe.

From elsewhere in the building: the wailing of a soul in distress, a fellow resident in a hopeless battle with himself. I remain staring at the far wall.

On the floor in corner of the room is a dark and unfamiliar shape. I try to bring it into focus but it resists, refusing even to reveal itself as something solid or merely a shadow. Frustrated that I cannot make it out I reluctantly leave my bed and step carefully over, my bare feet cold against the ground.

Squatting and placing my hands on either side of the object I find a sturdy wooden box, roughly a yard square with a lid and a metal clasp. I pick it up and give it a shake but hear nothing. Flicking back the clasp I lift the lid and put my hand inside, pressing down on the smooth base. It is empty.

Something brushes against my wrist. Instinctively I recoil, pulling my arm away and staring into the black space that seems only to grow blacker. Once my confidence is regained and my heartbeat has slowed I use the ends of my fingers to tip the lid shut. Taking the box to the window I place it on the floor. I open the shutters to let the moonlight in and carefully open the lid again.

Inside is a collection of house spiders. I don't know

what to make of this. There are roughly ten in number, in various stages of growth. Where have they come from? It must be a trick of some kind, an attempt to force me to question my sanity.

Hardy is the culprit, I am sure. He has taken a fierce dislike of me from the beginning and resents my wealth and my previous social standing.

Seeing one of the bigger spiders is threatening to escape I bring the lid down with a bang.

"You all right in there?" says the watcher.

"Fine, thank you."

*

Seward is in the doorway. Now more than ever I am perplexed by the time scales in which I exist. Sometimes I look out of the window in the belief that mere moments have passed only to see that the sun has shifted to the other side of the sky. On other occasions I have thought myself a prisoner in my room for weeks on end, then been told that no more time has passed than the gap between breakfast and dinner. I have no idea how long it has been since we last spoke.

"It is unhygienic," he is saying. "It will make you unwell."

With my back to him I sit on my chair and watch the flies race around the room. Currently there are thirty two in total. I know this because I have been keeping a careful log using the paper and notebook the doctor agreed to supply for me. I am also in possession of sixteen arachnids: ten common house spiders and six skull spiders.

My method of trapping the flies is simple. Attracted by the food festering in the sunshine they gather in great numbers on my sill. When plenty of guests have arrived at the banquet I pull down the window. My approach and the sash juddering in its frame disturbs them, of course, and I lose a great many to the outside world, but I usually manage to catch at least a few in the room. A second deposit of rotting food in the far corner is enough to keep most of my captives here when I reopen the window and begin my experiment again. Eventually these flies become meals for the spiders, half of which I keep in the box while the other half are allowed to roam the room, spinning their webs if and where they please.

"Please close the door behind you," I say to the Superintendent. "Quickly."

"I really am very sorry but I'm going to have to insist you remove them all."

I cast him a wounded look. My new doctor, I have learnt, is easier to manipulate than Carey.

He continues: "Or at least get rid of some of them, at all events."

"You are very kind to humour me."

"You have three days in which to do it. No more. I will not be swayed."

"Thank you," I swivel around in my chair to face him. "I have one more request, if I may."

"Go on."

"If it pleases you, I should like to be allowed out more often, and farther afield than the airing court. I am wasting away here. It does no good to be inactive. Exercise would benefit me both physically and mentally, I'm sure."

"You know I cannot allow you into the grounds just yet, Renfield. That's not to say it will never happen. We'll see how you progress."

A blowfly lands on my trouser leg: a healthy fellow, shiny and plump. I watch him scuttle and halt, scuttle and halt, seeking food. Fully expecting it to fly away I reach down and attempt to pinch it between my thumb and forefinger. To my great surprise, I succeed. My technique must be improving. Holding it up to my face I make a study of my catch, its one delicate wing crushed against its side while the other buzzes sporadically.

Seward comes further into the room: "Are they your pets? Do you mean to take care of them? Because flies and spiders cannot be cared for, you know. They're not that kind of animal."

Without thinking about it I pop the creature onto my tongue and close my mouth.

"Renfield! For heaven's sake, take that out."

It is too late for him to stop me. I have already swallowed it whole.

"What do you think you're doing?"

This is a very good question: "I am feeding myself, Doctor Seward. I would have thought that much was obvious."

"But why would you eat such a thing?" He bats a fly from in front of his nose. "It's revolting."

He is right. It is revolting and has left a deeply unpleasant after-taste: "This is very good and very wholesome food," I say, then try to suppress a cough.

"It is dirty and almost certainly bloated on carrion. Were you not, just a few moments ago, talking about the importance of physical health?"

"The fly is alive, Doctor. Therefore a life-giving thing. It stands to reason, wouldn't you agree? It's logical."

He frowns disapprovingly: "It is vile. Clear these animals away or I will arrange for it to be done for you."

*

I am one of forty in the airing court, hemmed in, disturbing the dust. Attendants stand over us, smoking and talking with key chains rattling on their belts. Pushed up against the brick walls which keep us from the unseen land beyond are a number of heavy wooden benches. It is on one of these I rest while an unfamiliar grey-haired attendant sips from the drinking fountain to my side. A short, balding inmate shuffles by, lost in some indecipherable monologue and watching his feet scrape incrementally forward.

Under the thatched roof of the shelter—the design of which is similar to those along the seafront at Plymouth–a group has formed, idiots mainly, drooling and contorting, while others act the part of the melancholic, scowling and shaking their miserable heads. One makes a remark that angers another and a messy scuffle breaks out, speedily quelled by our guardians but not before a sad-eyed chubby man receives a bloodied nose. Returning to his spot beside my bench the grey haired attendant calls over to a colleague in the hope of starting a conversation.

"We need a storm."

"Say again?"

"We need a storm. To clear the air. It's too muggy. Can you sleep at night? I can't get more than a few hours."

The other attendant shrugs and looks disinterestedly away. It occurs to me that since I was locked up my hay fever hasn't bothered me at all.

Perhaps the families of the night watchers were right. Perhaps the country is on the verge of a terrible plague, on the brink of catastrophe, just as David's American

107

showman friend predicted. Could the disease have already run its terrible course, spreading through our population by unknown and unstoppable means, leaving little but death in its wake? Piles of anonymous corpses burning in Regent's Park. Bodies disfigured by boils, breathing their last in Trafalgar Square. A mass exodus from the cities to the countryside where there are too few homes and too little food. A nation turning against itself, splitting into tribes. A bloody civil war. A dead island. How can any of us know for sure, locked away in this place? I eye the attendants with suspicion. Is it so far-fetched to imagine they are keeping the truth from us? Perhaps the incurable fever has spared only those who are cut off from society: the prison inmates and the asylum lunatics? Are we the only ones left? The morally dubious, the mentally corrupt, the physically ill? Are we destined to be the flawed and unwitting fathers of a new race?

A cloud passes in front of the sun and the air cools. How do I feel, I wonder? What is the apposite word?

Through a window on the top floor of the red brick madhouse I catch sight of a silhouette, a figure observing me through the glass. Is it Hardy? No, it is not Hardy. The cloud moves on and the glinting sunlight obscures the stranger.

'Expectant' is the word. I am 'expectant'.

Refreshed after a spell in the open I ask to be

accompanied to the door of my corridor, where the duty attendant uses his keys to let me inside. One of my fellow residents, to whom I never speak, is busy lighting his rationed cigarette from the gas-jet. He is smartly dressed with a neat and narrow moustache but his hands, I notice, are covered with brightly coloured paint. Without acknowledging him I approach my door, stopping in my tracks when I hear a disturbance from within. I look over my shoulder at the attendant and the smoker but they seem not to have noticed. The noise comes again: a frenzied rustle, something inhuman. I open the observation hatch but can see nothing unusual, only the zigzagging flies and the open window. Cautiously I turn the handle.

Perched on the headrest of my bed is a sparrow. A sparrow! Battling to escape it launches blindly at the wall, propelling itself up along the plaster and knocking against the bookshelf before dropping to the floor. Closing the door behind me I dash across the room and pull down the sash, sending a cloud of flies into the air. I must not let this opportunity slip.

Now the bird is trapped I sit down on my chair and rest my chin on my hand, captivated by its struggle: "Extraordinary."

Eventually and inevitably it runs out of strength and takes shelter against the wall at the end of my bed. This is far from the first time I have suspected my life is being manipulated by some outside force. What is this sparrow if not a sign and a gift? The box of spiders, I now see, was magically placed in my possession to aid me towards some unknown end. And now a bird has flown in through my window: the next step in the plan. Is this the work of God? Or some other force? Yet again I remember the silk-clad man who comforted me in the alleyway; the elderly gentleman spied by Miss Morley as he waited in the square outside my home.

Leaving my chair I crouch down beside my new pet and, watching its tiny frightened heart beating in its chest, take the exhausted creature in my hand.

＊

"I wonder if I am in the right place at all. I am here to be treated, correct? To be cured of some perceived antisocial trait? But what if I am not insane?"

Not long ago Hardy and Mr Simmons, the Principal Attendant, entered my room carrying a small table between them, on which stood what I recognised to be a modern phonograph. Seward followed soon after, with a chair and three neat folders of notes. Having made himself comfortable he prepared the equipment and told the attendants to leave us alone.

"You feel you have been imprisoned unjustly?" He has been attempting to grow a beard, without much success. Blonde wisps of hair are faintly visible below his nose and on his chin. "Because if the court was incorrect it must follow that you attacked your victim in full possession of your senses."

"If you accept that I attacked anyone, yes, but I do not. I have no memory of it and therefore no reason to believe it."

"Then why were you sent here?"

"To be punished, I suppose. Not by the crown or the court but something greater, something entirely inescapable…. Forgive me, I find this difficult to speak about…" I take a moment to choose my words. "I am in state of sin, doctor: a state in need of constant purging and redress. All my life I have been plagued by lascivious thoughts that come quite unbidden and are hard to reject. Even as a child in Ceylon I was fascinated by the Indian girls who played all day in the sand. I was obsessed by their nakedness and their coffee coloured skin. Is it not possible that my whole existence is a deserved form of punishment? Do not misunderstand me; I am not claiming this as the truth. I am simply offering a possible explanation drawn from a clear-eyed and objective observation of my circumstances."

Seward listens and nods thoughtfully and scribbles

111

down his notes: "I have been pondering something you mentioned yesterday. Do you remember? About gaining nourishment from living things. Is this something you still believe?"

The brown wax cylinder silently spins, recording not only our words but also the hammering from outside: roofers making repairs. Wishing to make my ideas understood I speak loudly and distinctly towards the mouth of the phonograph's horn.

"Yes, that is what I believe."

"Would you care to elaborate? It is your opinion that when one living creature eats another a transference of some kind of life force, like a soul, takes place?"

"Is it not obvious?"

"The scientific community would stand against that theory."

"Whatever the consensus, I would suggest there is a clear difference between taking something dead into your belly and consuming a living being, rich with energy."

"Maybe so, but not with regards to the level of sustenance it provides."

"Honestly, Seward, is it too much to hope that an asylum Superintendent can grasp such a childishly simple notion?" He glances at me over the rim of his spectacles. Seeing I have spoken too harshly I change my tone. It will do no good to turn this young man against me. "I apologise, I don't wish to be insulting. I only mean to say that if someone like me understands it–a lowly prisoner in a madhouse-then I would expect someone of your superior intellect to understand it too."

He nudges his spectacles farther up the bridge of his nose. It is a new pair, with black frames rather than gold ones: "And all creatures have souls? Not only humans but lesser beings? Flies, for example?"

"Flies, yes. Or woodlice, or worms. All creatures. The larger ones providing more nourishment."

"I see. Can I ask how you came about this information?"

"Instinct and simple scientific deduction. The concept seems so obvious now I can hardly believe it took me so long to acknowledge it."

We are both distracted by a scratching noise coming from under my bed. The sparrow hops into sight.

"Birds too?" says Seward, expressing no surprise. "They have souls?"

"Naturally."

A quizzical frown forms on his face: "Why is this one unable to fly, Renfield?"

"It's wings are broken."

"How did they break?"

"It is properly fed. I make sure of that."

"You feed it with spiders?"

"That's correct."

113

"How did it get in here?"

"It flew through the window."

"Is it your pet?"

"Yes. My pet."

The wax cylinder has run out of space. Apologising for the interruption Seward sets about replacing it.

"While you're here, doctor," I say, "I have one more request. You have amply demonstrated your generosity by providing me with a new notebook and pencil..."

"Go on."

"I should like something else to take care of. A new pet. A kitten."

He looks doubtful.

"A nice, sleek, playful grey kitten," I say. "For me to teach and feed."

A fly settles on the shoulder of the doctor's coat and he distractedly brushes it away: "I am sorry Renfield, but at the present time I am unsure that's going to be possible. I will see about it, though. I promise you that."

This answer fills me with a sudden, hot rage. Who is this little boy to refuse me? I should grab him by his fragile throat and crack his head against the table, thrust my thumbs into his eye sockets and smash his skull. I remind myself to be calm. There is much to be achieved first.

The doctor stirs, unsettled. It seems I was too slow in keeping my emotions from my face. Hoping to repair the

114

damage I offer him a smile but he is already gathering his folders and getting to his feet: "Two more days to clean all this filth up, Renfield. Thank you for your time."

Leaving his machine to be collected by the attendants he goes out into the corridor where he is obstructed by Hardy, who asks if he has a moment to spare. I lie back on my bed and listen.

"Is there a problem?"

"All this talk of a plague on its way, sir. I wanted to ask if you thought there was anything in it, being an educated man. My wife's beside herself with worry."

"A plague? It's possible, of course, but I doubt it."

"Our grocer was taken ill just a few days ago."

"Hardly an uncommon occurrence, is it?"

"No, but still. Mrs Hardy has hung a charm by the baby's cot, just to be safe."

"With respect, Mr Hardy, do you honestly suppose a few scraps of scented ribbon can repel a disease? You shouldn't worry so much. It sounds to me as if the only infection being passed around is superstition. One individual gets it in their head that a terrible plague is coming and soon enough the fear is repeated in the imagination of their neighbours, and their neighbours after that. Use the charm if it comforts you but don't waste your energy fretting. Tell your wife everything will be fine."

It is once night has fallen and my door has been locked

that I suffer another influx of light.

*

When I regain consciousness I am on the floor, on my front with my head to one side. My chair has been tipped over and my mattress upturned. I take a deep breath and resolve to stay perfectly still until I am healthy and safe.

Without warning a sudden contraction grips my stomach, so painful it pulls my body into a tight ball. It is impossible to call for help.

When the agony resides I struggle to my hands and knees, knowing I am about to vomit. Has Hardy administered some kind of strong emetic while I was knocked out? I puke with such violence I am afraid I might bring up my insides: once, twice. Almost too scared to look I open my watery eyes. A green and red mess covers my hands and the floor. Blinking, I see strange shapes mixed up in the liquid. It takes a few moments before I make out what they are. Feathers, claws, and a beak.

Another contraction strikes and I roll onto my side. I barely recognise the sounds my throat has begun to produce as my own. A long high wail, an animal in distress. It is hard to breathe. What have I been doing while I was unconscious? Did I become something less than human?

The night watcher is in the room, trying to hold me

down and calling for assistance. I fight against him but my body is weak. Once I have been restrained a second man enters, then a third: a physician with a briefcase. After rolling up the sleeve of my nightgown he slips a needle into the crook of my arm. Then, nothing.

... I am looking down at what appears to be a scaled down model of my room, with four walls but no ceiling. The bed has been intricately constructed using thin sticks tied together with woollen threads. The upturned chair is made from trimmed matches and a bottle cap. By the door sits the spider box, now no larger than my thumb nail. A low, persistent wind blows outside.

A small bundle of rags shifts on the floor. Regarding it closely I recognise it as a miniature version of myself, dressed in a nightgown. Oblivious to my gaze my tiny doppelganger gets to his feet, replaces the chair in the centre of the floor and sits down.

Something raps on the window shutter, three times in quick succession: knock, knock, knock. Lost in his thoughts, Little Renfield seems not to hear. The rapping comes again. This time he looks up but does not move. For a long time there is no sound except the deep rumbling of the wind. Finally there follows a third set of raps.

"Go away," we say, both Little Renfield and I. Turning

117

his back on the shutter he covers his ears with his hands.

The rapping turns to scratching, travelling slowly down from the window to the outside of the wall, then beneath the floor. Resisting whatever force pushes against them the boards bend and creak. The bulge inches this way and that, searching for a weak spot. Blocking it out, Little Renfield stares ahead until eventually the shape moves under the bed and falls silent.

Something is emerging from beneath the sheets: a child's hand and forearm. Terrified, Little Renfield jumps up, toppling his chair, and runs towards the intruder, shouting and kicking wildly. Before he can make contact the hand pulls back and vanishes. Slowing backing away, Renfield retrieves his chair and sits down again, fidgeting with the material of his nightgown.

Another hand is reaching out from closer to the head of the bed. It is joined by a third, then a forth. Soon there are more than twenty slender hands extending slowly into the room. Little Renfield grabs the bottle-cap chair and launches it at them. Acting as one, they retract and disappear.

More scratching and scuffling and the bulge below the floorboards rolls out from under the bed then back up outside the window shutter. Over the sound of the wind come three distinct raps: knock, knock, knock.

Little Renfield has been taunted enough. In one swift

118

and decisive movement he paces bravely to the shutter and flings it open, revealing nothing but the dark blue of the night sky. Relieved, he bends down and rests his hands on his knees.

All at once the model begins to shake. Dozens of children are scaling the outside walls. They wear dirty long-johns and have wild hair and long fingernails and sharp teeth. Over the top they clamber, into the room, joining streams of other children from through the window and beneath the bed, hundreds of them. Little Renfield cowers, uselessly putting up a defence as they rush ceaselessly toward him. They claw and bite at his shivering body, his arms, his chest, his neck.

Unnoticed in the corner, the spider box flips open, as if the lid has been yanked by an invisible thread. From within a huge, hairy, searching limb appears: the leg of a spider, large from my perspective but immense within the confines of the model. Improbably the creature manages to squeeze its swollen abdomen through the gap and crawls towards the ever growing pile of children, its legs tapping and twitching. Little Renfield is buried, his screams no longer audible.

A flare of brilliant white blinds me before I am once again plunged into a void...

... Much, much later a single pin point of light appears,

unique in the expanse. In time, a second light appears, orange tinged and wavering. It is warm and friendly, a presence reassuring enough to quell my fears. I try to lift my hand to my face but I cannot find it. No hand. No face. No body at all. Only two lights and nothingness.

Gradually—so, so gradually—I become aware that the expanse is not empty at all but filled by a vast and multicoloured array of stars. Constellations of every imaginable shape and size begin to reveal themselves. A whole universe around and within me. All of creation, all time, all of a piece.

One of the stars is significantly brighter than the others, like a marker or a waypoint. If I concentrate I can see it is becoming brighter still, slowly gathering strength... No, not gathering strength, but drawing closer.

If it is coming to meet me it has a long way to travel. Its progress is so slight it is barely discernible. More than a millennium passes before it has even doubled in size. I am content to wait. Having no body I cannot grow old, or fall ill, or die. In every direction stars are born and are extinguished, while solar systems swell and disperse: as if the universe is breathing.

Countless lifetimes go by. I begin to make out a shape in the approaching star. The object is not circular as I had thought, but humanoid. By the time it has completed a quarter of its journey I can see it is a naked woman, silvery skinned with straight black hair hanging over her shoulders. Halfway closer still and I see she is opening and closing her mouth, as if she is singing, although she is too far away for me to hear her voice. For this I must wait another billion years.

Only when she is close enough, when I am looking into her glazed milky white eyes and can feel her breath on my face, am I rewarded with a sound so quiet as to be almost undetectable but still entirely human. It is pure and intelligent and achingly beautiful.

On she comes and nothing is left in my field of vision but her mouth, her perfect white teeth and glistening tongue. Compared to her I am nothing: bacteria; a mote of dust. At the back of her throat I glimpse something unexpected: a black polished shape like a beetle's shell. This, too, draws closer as the woman envelopes me, taking the whole of me inside her cavernous mouth. I was mistaken: it is not a shell but the horn of a phonograph, the source of the singing voice. The sound is so unguarded and simple it breaks my heart.

At length the mouth of the horn swallows me too and I am left hanging in emptiness with nothing but the song. Finally it weakens and dies, as all things must...

... The smell of burning coal. I am in my chair at home by the hearth. David is sat opposite me, a glass of wine in one hand and his cherry-wood pipe in the other. Outside the window fog swirls under the street lights. Miss Morley clatters pans in the kitchen downstairs.

"David," I say.

He has aged little since we last met. His hair is as untameable and his eyebrows as arched as ever. Lit by the crackling fire he breaks into an easy smile.

"David," I say. "I'm so glad you're here."

He looks as if he is about to reply but thinks better of it. Again he smiles, more to himself than to me. Somehow sensing I may not be here for very long I resolve to make the most of my visit and settle into my old familiar seat, enjoying the leather creaking under my weight. A full glass of red is waiting for me on the table. I pick it up and take a sip. Outside, the fog continues to swirl.

David coughs to get my attention and nods at something over my shoulder. I ask him what he wants me to do. He nods again.

Looking behind me I see a large mahogany wardrobe taken from my bedroom, crammed into the corner and completely blocking the bookshelves.

"Did you move that? Thank you, but I think I preferred it where it was. It's of no use to me here."

My companion takes the pipe from his mouth and points the stem at the round-cornered doors.

"You want me to open it?"

I get up, cross the rug and take hold of the brass handles. A formidable presence waits for me within, something dark and heavy, something massive enough to distort time. I brace myself and pull.

What confronts me is a solid wall of mud. A scattering of loose dirt falls to the carpet but otherwise it is packed in tightly, filling the space's every inch. I look to David for an explanation but he is busy savouring his tobacco and displays no interest. I scratch the surface with my forefinger and more dirt falls away. Diligently rolling up my shirt sleeves I briefly notice a small puncture wound in the crook of my arm. Then I grab a fistful and let it drop. Miss Morley will be angry with me in the morning but I have no choice. Using of both hands now I dig out a hole. Before I know it I am up to my elbows, then my shoulders, burrowing like a dog and pushing towards the back. When the hole is sufficiently wide I place my knee on its lip and haul myself inside.

The glossy mud reaches farther than I had anticipated, far beyond where the bookshelves should be. Soon I am able to stretch my entire body out flat with no trouble at all. More and more deeply I delve, excavating as I go, the tunnel collapsing in my wake. I dig around rocks, and pipes, and the roots of trees. Then, just as I think I will never come to the end, I see sunlight.

The soil around my fingers crumbles away and fresh air

rushes in. With surprising ease I am able to lift myself from the ground, disoriented to find I have been digging not horizontally, but vertically. Brambles scratch my head and torso as I push through them. The dirt on my face is too thick for me to see but wherever I am the air is damp and cool. Once I am free I take a few deep breaths then wipe my eyes.

I am under a darkening sky, surrounded by tall trees. My clothes are torn and caked with mud. My hands are bleeding. I wonder how far I am from a town or a place where I can shelter. Looking down at my feet I see I have lost my shoes and socks. I clench my toes and release, clench and release.

I see am being watched. Two children stand in the low lying fog, a boy and a girl, roughly twelve years of age. The girl has black curly hair and wears a white dress. The boy is athletically built with a long face, like my father's. Taking fright on encountering me—a broken-down, bleeding vagrant in the woods—the girl turns and flees. Before following her, the boy meets my eyes, communicating a flicker of vague recognition.

I am alone and the light is dying fast. From somewhere on my right comes a familiar noise, like the snapping of fingers or the clucking of a tongue. Turning towards it I see nothing but a dense veil of mist. Could my senses be deceiving me? Are these just the natural sounds of the forest reflecting from the trees? I look again and the mist is clearing, partly unveiling what I first take to be an enormous and muscular black dog, the size of a horse. The mist thickens and the shape changes.

Stepping towards me is an elderly man, seven foot tall at the least, with agile, slender limbs and a long white moustache hanging down either side of his mouth. His skin is pale, his lips are red. His costume is speckless, black from head to toe. With his manifestation comes a powerful smell of rotting vegetation. I know who he is. We have met before.

"Poor Renfield," he says, a simple expression of sympathy that brings me trembling and weeping to my knees. He speaks but doesn't speak. "Do you know my name?"

I do. I have known it for as long as I can remember.

"It is time. Do you understand?"

I understand completely and with all my heart.

Without a sound he treads through the brambles, the silver top of a wooden cane in his hand. The ground beneath his feet ripples like water. All around, the birds of the forest have woken and are calling to each other.

"I know how hard this has been for you. I know what you have endured, how terribly you suffered. Look at you. Humiliated, foul, unable even to speak."

I look into the old man's eyes. They are shining, black

and inscrutable, like those of a sea creature.

"I promise you though, it has not been for nothing. As gruelling as your trials have been, they were necessary to lead you here."

Placing his arms around my neck he draws me to him, laying his cold cheek to mine and murmuring into my ear. The birds are in a frenzy, their squawks a dreadful cacophony.

"Soon," he says. "Soon you will be magnificent."

PART THREE

I clear away the rotting food and release the blowflies. The spiders I tip out of the window from their wooden box, watching them tumbling sideways, carried by the wind. Their purpose—to teach me about the sustenance one living animal can gain from consuming another—has been served. I have no further need for them. On the distant horizon the thin line of trees look black against the grey sky.

I feel healthy and purged. It excites me to imagine what might happen now. What form will the next stage of my renewal take? Am I to be sent instructions, by means of another vision, or thought transference? Or will my course be signposted by gifts, just as happened with the spiders and the sparrow? If I am impatient it is only because I am keen to do my saviour's bidding. I am sure he understands. I shove the box in the bottom of my wardrobe.

When Seward arrives I am sat on the edge of my bed trying to empty my mind of thoughts, hoping to prevent the obstruction of any psychic communications. Disappointingly, my request for a pot of green tea instead of dinner was ignored and I was given chicken and vegetables. I ate the vegetables but left the meat, finding I

129

could barely stand to have it on my plate: a dead lump in thin gravy, decaying from the moment the animal was killed, providing no nourishment at all.

"Thank you for cleaning up your room as I asked."

Annoyed by the distraction I keep my mouth shut.

"Don't you feel better? More wholesome? Living in such squalor could only have worsened your condition."

It is impossible to block out his chatter: "Yes, but please be assured, it was not done for your sake."

"I'm glad to hear you're taking responsibility for your own surroundings."

"That is not what I meant. Is it really necessary for you to speak so much?"

He takes a seat on my chair: "We have never discussed what happened when you relocated to England from Ceylon. Godalming's notes mention you lived with your uncle. Is that right?"

"What of it?"

"Do you remember much about him? Was he good to you?"

"I remember a great deal about him. He took me into his home, at my father's request, without hesitation. Of course he was good to me."

"Did it upset you that your father sent you away?"

"Not in the least. Our school could only ever have taken me so far. I needed to be given a formalised education. I will admit that coming to a new country with an unfamiliar climate and culture was jarring at first but I adapted soon enough. Pragmatism is one of the traits I inherited from my father."

My earliest years were spent on a missionary settlement in Manepy, passing many of my days as any young boy would be expected to in such idyllic surroundings: racing to the tops of Sadikka trees and splashing about in the ocean. What hazy memories remain of this period are mainly populated by Indian girls in straw-roofed huts, backgrounded by golden horseshoe beaches and a cobalt sea. I spent most of my time alone, my younger sister Dora only being of interest to me as an occasional target for bullying.

When I was roughly five, too young to fully understand what had happened, my mother died of consumption. A few years later my father-a practical man by all accounts-took it upon himself to find a new wife and, seeing no possible candidates in our station, took me with him for an exploratory trip through the Malay Peninsula. Dora, being laid up in the Green Memorial Hospital with a mild bout of malaria, was left in the care of a Dutch missionary family of our acquaintance (the father of whom had taught me a few words of their first language). As it happened, I never saw her again. While we were away her adopted family moved to Bangkok where she reportedly succumbed to the same deadly disease that had taken our mother.

My father and I were staying in Singapore when he met an American named Sylvia. Somehow he persuaded her to leave the Christian church group with whom she was travelling and return to Manepy as his wife. She was a shy woman and did not make friends easily, preferring whenever possible to communicate through my father. I never got to know my new stepmother very well and suspect she was never fond of me: an arrangement which suited me perfectly. My concerns lay elsewhere.

One might imagine a boy's education would suffer in these circumstances but the missionary school was of the highest standard and its library stocked with a surprisingly varied and impressive range. It was here that my passion for learning was first aroused. By the age of ten, with little help from my teacher, I was fluent in Sinhalese, and had developed a workable grasp of Burmese, Hindi, and Tamil. I had read more novels than any of the adults on the settlement, leaving my classmates far behind. I wrote, too: poems and a journal and any number of stories. But it was the sciences which took the strongest hold over me. Sitting under the trees outside the library while Ceylon Lorikeets called to each other I devoured books on botany, geology, zoology, astronomy: whatever I could find. Assisted by my father I became a keen lepidopterist, taking advantage of the jungle to build my collection and diligently pinning my specimens to cork boards which I displayed in my bedroom.

Twice in my life I have been guilty of stealing: once a few years later, when I stole a knife from my a drawer in our kitchen in Yorkshire, and once when, at the age of ten, I slipped a favourite entomology text under my shirt to take with me on my solo trip to England. Only minutes before my father had visited the library to tell me he was sending me away to live with his brother. Sylvia had come with him but she wandered off part way through the conversation. My ship wasn't due to sail for another fortnight but taking possession of the book seemed like an immediate priority, whatever the risk. Who knew whether a copy would be available in Whitby, or even anything similar? Leaving my father and my home seemed tolerable, even exciting. Leaving my favourite book was unacceptable. If the librarian saw me sneak between the shelves and remove it he didn't say anything.

"Do you think your uncle ever resented taking you in?" says Seward. "Especially after he was invalided. That's what happened, isn't it?"

"I'm not sure I care for the question. Of course he wasn't resentful. He relished the opportunity to guide me, to pass on his values. My uncle was an extraordinary man: driven, disciplined, fiercely principled. Even after he had been robbed of his physical robustness. I like to think I have taken after him. Far more than my father, he made me into the man I am today."

The doctor wanders over to the window and runs his hand over the newly cleaned sill. Dark patches, I notice, circle his tired eyes and he has shaved off his unimpressive beard. He is restless, filling in time: "Was it easy to put everything in order? Did it take long to clear out your pets?"

He suspects I have eaten them: "Bother them all. I don't care a pin about them."

"You mean to say you never cared for them? Even after I went to all the trouble of providing me with that box? It wasn't easy to find, you know."

"The box?"

"Yes. The wooden box I gave you. You were very pleased. Do you not remember?"

Before I have a chance to respond something swells in my chest, pushing my words out of the way and forcing itself irresistibly up into my throat and out of my mouth: "The Bride maidens," I blurt, somewhat startled. I do not know what I am saying.

"What was that?"

"The Bride maidens. They rejoice the eyes that wait the coming of the bride. But when the bride draweth nigh then the maidens shine not to the eyes that are filled."

"What do you mean? Are you quoting scripture?"

*

Only hours later, when Seward has taken his leave and I have changed into my nightgown and climbed into bed, am I struck by the meaning of these words. It is a message, of course, a message from my master and saviour, delivered in the form of a riddle. Staring hard at the far wall I attempt to unpick it. It stands to reason that I am the 'one who waits'. Therefore my saviour must be the bride that draws near. But who are the bride maidens? Are they the attendants? My fellow inmates? I sit up and pull my legs towards me.

The solution strikes like a thunderbolt. The maidens represent knowledge. Knowledge will not be imparted to anyone whose eyes are filled. So I will not receive my message if I am awake. In such a state of exhilaration it will be difficult for me to fall asleep but I lay back and close my eyes….

A vision: the outer boundary of the airing court. Above the wall the sky is cloudless and the moon is three-quarters full. At first nothing seems out of place but if I concentrate I can see a portion of brickwork has become distorted, misty, as if something opaque hangs before it. An extraordinary intelligence is calling out to me. I must find a way to reach it.

Shoving my bed sheets away I go to the shutter and quietly push up the window. Surly it is too high to jump? From this perspective, here on the second floor, the patchy grass below seems dauntingly distant. Although I was not witness to the event I remember hearing of an inmate who tried the same thing and shattered the bones in both his legs, leaving him unable to walk. I must consider this logically; employ my trained scientist's mind. Struck by an idea I put on my shoes without bothering with socks or changing out of my nightgown. Then I strip my bed and heave the mattress to the window, folding it in the middle and giving it a series of shoves with my shoulder to force it through. It hits the ground with a hollow thud. Gathering my resolve I take hold of either side of the frame and clamber onto the sill. After taking a few seconds to prepare myself I launch into the chilly night air.

The fall lasts for an age. I hit the mattress heavily, turning my ankle and landing on my right side. Winded and gasping for breath I struggle to my feet. I cannot afford to hesitate. Down the space between the two high walls I limp, every step sending a pain shooting up my right leg. At the corner of the building I am forced to rest for a moment before pushing onwards.

Seen at night the airing court seems unfamiliar to me, far larger now without the shuffling and nonsense of the lunatics. Unlit windows look down over the wooden benches. From a distance I scan the patch of wall that appeared to be distorted in my vision, but see nothing unusual. I move closer, passing through the thatched shelter. Still nothing. The brief moment of black despair this brings about is quickly swept away when I realise the apparition must have been meant as a marker, a waypoint, like the North Star. My saviour wishes for me to not only break the confines of my room, but of Carfax itself. This is the spot at which I will make my escape.

Taking the nearest bench by the armrest I begin to drag it behind me, pleased to discover that my time in the asylum has yet to sap all my former physical strength. I must work quickly: the sound of the feet scraping along the floor is sure to draw attention. Pushing the backrest against the wall I climb onto the seat but find the top is still far out of my reach, as I worried it might be. I look around for something else to use as a boost but find nothing suitable. In an act of desperation I stretch my arms up and discover, to my amazement, that I am able to place my hands comfortably over the creasing tiles. It is nothing less than a miracle. My saviour has shortened the distance, extended the bones in my arms, manipulating the laws of the universe to assist me on my journey. I have no time to reflect on the enormity of this. Placing the soles of my feet against the bricks I haul myself over and drop down the other side, grazing my palms on the way.

How long has it been since I was last outside the walls of the asylum? Long enough for me to sincerely doubt whether the world beyond even exists. And yet here it is, undeniably before me: a narrow mud track leading to my left and to my right, lined by thick brambles heavy with fruit. Farther down the path a fox stands frozen with one paw raised as it assesses the level of threat I present. We stare at each other, my ankle throbbing exquisitely. Once the glossy-coated creature is satisfied that I mean no harm it turns and trots nonchalantly away. In equal measure terrified and exhilarated by my new found freedom I obey my instincts and follow the trail to the left.

I am led down the slope, across some train tracks, and eventually to a place where the path opens up, taking me to a medieval church with a small, walled graveyard. Looking back I see the moonlit Gothic madhouse perched on the top of the hill and become convinced—*convinced*—that I should be able to see the church tower from my room. But the construction is entirely new to me. Where could it have materialised from, this moss covered and crumbling structure? Has it been conjured into existence for my benefit? My saviour is more powerful than I could ever have imagined, and my mission one of unparalleled importance. Pushing through the iron gate I hobble along the grass-grown stone path.

The doors are padlocked and chained. There must be

another way inside. As I circumnavigate the building I am shocked by a sudden and ear-splitting noise: the escape sirens are sounding, a long wail descending downwind. My absence has been detected. I must work quickly. The rear door of the church, I discover, is also bolted, and every one of the stained glass windows protected with thick wire mesh. I am at a loss. In the distance people are calling to each other, organising an approach.

"I am here to do your bidding," I whisper. If I cannot break into the church I must try to communicate with my saviour by other means. "I am your slave, and you will reward me, for I will be faithful. I have worshipped you long and afar off."

I wait for a reply but nothing comes.

Four watchers are visible now, the silver buttons of their uniforms flashing in the moonlight. Having spread themselves strategically they approach from different directions, one through the gate, one by way of the tower, and two stepping carefully around the tombstones.

In desperation I continue my plea: "Now that you are near, I await your commands. And you will not pass me by, will you, dear Master, in your distribution of good things?"

From ten yards away one of the watchers breaks into a run towards me. Swinging my weight around I meet his jaw with my fist and send him collapsing to the ground. My task is incomplete and I must not be obstructed.

Taking me by surprise a second watcher grabs me around the neck from behind and works to pin back my arms. In response I stamp on his feet and elbow him in the gut. He doubles over and lets me go but I am rammed violently from the side and sent sprawling.

Knees on my spine. A palm pushing my head down. Lichen on a burial slab scratching my cheek. Hardy is on top of me, his face contorted with pleasure and rage.

"Got you now," he spits.

A ferocious bite to his thumb causes him to rear away. I fight to get upright but barely make it to my feet before I am caught again, this time around the waist. Dealing a blow to my assailant's nose I feel the bone crack beneath my fist but ultimately I am overpowered and bundled into the long grass. All four men are needed to hold me down.

It is an opportunity too sweet for Hardy to resist. Pulling back his fist he drives it into my face: once, twice, three times. He will kill me if he is not stopped.

"Enough!"

Seward's voice, somewhere nearby.

"That's enough!"

Too keyed-up to hear, Hardy continues his attack while his colleagues keep me pinned. The escape sirens howl.

"He is a *patient!*"

The Superintendent pulls him off me and Hardy steps away, his fist covered with blood that may or may not be

140

my own: "He was asking for it. He struck the first blow."

After a brief spell in the Infirmary I am taken to a padded cell, buckled into a straight waistcoat and shackled to the wall.

*

My uncle's housekeeper in Whitby was of a different species. No taller than a child but as broad and round as a barrel, she had a prominent black mole protruding from her chin and hair so thin the grey skin of her scalp was visible. Rather than walk she waddled, her tiny steps punctuated by high pitched wheezes. From my perspective Mrs Highsmith seemed ancient, unimaginable as a younger woman, although in retrospect I suppose she was somewhere between fifty and sixty years of age.

Standing next to her it was difficult not to think myself superior, both physically and mentally. Her forgetfulness was a source of frustration to my uncle as much as me, especially when his reliance on her suddenly increased following the sharp downturn in his health. She was forever spoiling food by leaving it too long in the oven, or neglecting to prepare my bath. Worse, she seemed unable to stop herself from addressing me as John, no matter how angry it made me. Oscar explained she once had a son of that name who had perished in the Opium War, so

I should try my best to be patient with her. Evidently I looked a lot like him.

I was studying the etymology text I had stolen from the library in Manepy when she came into the dining room to tell me I was to see my uncle in his private study straight away. It embarrassed me to be in her company. Just before I woke that morning she had featured in one of the lascivious dreams that had plagued me all summer. It was a habit of mind which I seemed unable to prevent. That she had come to be the subject of one these unwelcome fantasies was, I suppose, something to do with her being the only grown woman who I encountered on a regular basis, but this made is no less shameful.

"Hurry along now, John" she said. "You know very well he wouldn't want to be kept waiting."

This could only be bad news. Uncle Patrick seldom spoke to me after our evening meal, and never invited me into his study unless he intended to dole out some punishment. What could I have done? My heart sank when I remembered the glass beaker I had accidentally broken the previous week. It had cracked when I dropped it and rather than admit my fault I had washed it and placed it in the kitchen cupboard with the crack turned the other way. Preparing myself for a rebuke I passed Mrs Highsmith in the doorway and made my way upstairs.

Although it had been three years since I moved to

Yorkshire my uncle's study was still an unfamiliar place, only ever entered in his presence and by invitation. Inside, any wall space not taken up by books and trophies was packed by double-hung landscapes, many of which had been painted by Patrick's father, my grandfather. Dominating an entire corner was a piano. As well as being a keen sportsman my uncle was a talented amateur musician, a gift mercifully unaffected by his malady. He took great pleasure in playing at night and I often went to sleep accompanied by the sound. About Beethoven he was evangelical, reciting his pieces without the aid of sheet music. Although he claimed to have no favourite compositions he played Piano Sonata No.14 more than any other.

I knocked on the door and waited to be admitted.

"Come in."

I found my uncle positioned in his red leather armchair, dressed in his *robe de chambre* and with his familiar old cane resting against the shelves to his side. In the firelight his eyes appeared even more sunken than usual.

"Richard. Sit down."

I did as I was told, placing myself on the mahogany-framed sofa that backed onto the opposite wall, still unsure whether I would admit to my deception or deny all knowledge.

"Richard." He seemed restive, less sure of himself than

usual. "I had a disturbing conversation with Oscar this morning." The blood drained from my face. "I am sure you know what it concerned. Your antics with Magdalene. To say I am disappointed would be understate myself. I am…" He took a moment to find the appropriate expression. "Disgusted. How old are you, boy?"

"I am thirteen, sir."

"Thirteen. And are you a child of God?"

"Yes, sir."

This was the worst thing imaginable. To have my true condition exposed. He rubbed his thumb and forefinger together, a small gesture that betrayed a barely repressed fury: "I wonder if you are. I wonder."

For a time we sat in silence, the fire crackling in the hearth. The urge to defend myself was strong. I wished to deny the kiss ever happened, to insist Oscar was either mistaken or lying, but I was afraid to disappoint him even further.

"I'm sorry."

He leans forward in is chair and roars, the spit gathering in the corners of his lips. His cane topples to the floor with a dull clump: "Don't you dare speak!"

I stare at the carpet, seeing ghoulish faces in the pattern. My uncle settles back and composes himself.

"It made me sick to hear it. Have I taught you nothing about physical purity? I am quite at a loss how to deal with this. Maybe you are beyond help. Maybe your soul is already blackened. You are fallen. Filthy." He sighs. "Anyway. You will not be seeing Magdalene again and there will be no more trips to the river. You are too old for such things as it is. Now, go to bed."

*

My cell is tall and narrow, with yellowish Indian rubber covering the floor and reaching three-quarters of the way up to the ceiling. There is a small window in the top corner, with a latch which is far out of my reach. I am now a resident of the Strong Block: locked up, dangerous, violent.

During the daytime, when the sun is up, I have nothing in my heart but anger. Only the jacket and the chains around my ankles prevent me from murdering the men who mean to keep me from my destiny. Something at the centre of me gets lost in the rage and I enter a non-human state, closer to a beast than to a man, where there is no future or past, no capacity or need to form memories. All that matters is the present moment and the fight against my bonds. When I emerge and become myself again awake my legs are invariably cut and bruised where I have struggled against my shackles. Often I have soiled my clothes. Only when the moon is shining through the tiny window am I able to believe my saviour will soon be at hand.

It is night-time when Seward comes to see me. He keeps his distance, out of my reach. I am sat on the floor, my chin down against my chest.

"Why did you try to escape?" he asks. He looks tired, overworked, depleted, as if he hasn't been sleeping. "I wish you hadn't. And I wish you hadn't fought back. None of this would have been necessary."

Taking my time before answering I run my bruised tongue delicately over the swelling inside my cheek, tensing at the sudden pain: "I did not merely *try* to escape. I succeeded."

"True enough, but it wasn't for long."

"Not long enough."

He squats near the door so he can speak at my level: "The men have been suitably disciplined. And you won't be seeing Hardy any more. He has been moved onto other duties."

"A pity. I should have relished some time alone with him."

"At the graveyard," he says. "You were talking to someone. Who was it?"

"So the graveyard was real? You could see it too?"

"Yes. Why do you think I might not have been able to?"

"It doesn't matter. In response to your first question: it is no business of yours who I was speaking to."

"You are aware you were alone, yes? There was nobody with you."

"Nobody outside the church. Nobody who could be seen."

"There was someone inside?"

"Enough questions, Seward. I have neither the energy nor the inclination."

He runs his hand through his sandy hair then stands, straightening the line of his trousers as he does so: "Very well. I can see we shall get nowhere tonight."

Once he has gone I slip into a shallow sleep.

*

Confronted with my mental weaknesses I was forced to withdraw. Being in the company of my uncle proved intolerable. My hands shook, my face flushed. He had glimpsed a dark shameful part of me and I could hardly stand it. Over our meals we barely spoke. On hearing the click of his cane as he approached on one of his regular strolls around the house I would quietly shut the door, or make myself scarce.

My relationship with Mrs Highsmith was no better. Paranoid that my uncle might have told her what I had done I sensed disapproval in everything she said or did. Worse, my dreams about her had not stopped. If anything, they had become more vivid, so that when we crossed paths during the day I experienced a confusing mixture of repulsion and attraction. It was easier to avoid her wherever possible. Sometimes I was able to distract myself with my books but most of the time I merely worried and brooded.

I wondered if Magdalene had been treated the same way by Oscar. Would she feel as ashamed as I? Given her increasingly forthright personality I found it hard to imagine: she would dismiss the accusation as easily as batting a fly from her collar. From time to time I believed I might be capable of the same disregard but my confidence soon faded.

A week had passed since my humiliation. Hearing a knock at my bedroom door I momentarily imagined it might be Mrs Highsmith come to visit me before bed, but it was Uncle Patrick in his nightgown, holding what appeared to be a weighty bundle of leather and metal. Although we had not spoken since breakfast he put aside any greetings and launched abruptly into what he wished to say.

"I feel I may have spoken to you too harshly. This is not to say I excuse what you did. I have had some time to ponder the matter and have come to the conclusion that addressing you in such a way could only be counterproductive. I would have hoped my many years as a leader in the Volunteer movement would have taught me the best way to communicate with young men, but there you have it: we are, none of us, perfect. So, seeing as I am currently your sole guardian I have decided instead to offer my support and do whatever I can to steer you back onto the right track. I have purchased this for you."

I accepted the bundle of material and held it out in front of me. It was something like a corset with a riveted steel band around the waist, attached to a metal cup and tube.

"I got the idea from a book I was reading on boy's health. It is designed to help you focus your mind. I think it should be fairly obvious how you put it on. I will be back in a few minutes to tighten it for you."

He closed the door behind him and I undressed. Turning the garment around a few times—it was heavier than it looked—I located the armholes and put the steel band around over my hips. The cup, I now saw, was to cover my genitals, making them inaccessible to me. My penis went inside the tube.

Uncle Patrick returned and placed his cane on my bedside table before tugging the corset strings - "Is this comfortable? Can you breathe easily?" -and locking the steel band at the back.

"There, you see?" The device was secure and impossible for me to remove without his assistance. "Now you shall be free from unnecessary distractions."

I slipped my nightgown over my head and climbed into bed. When I was settled he touched my forehead. It was the most affectionate gesture he had ever made towards me: lightly brushing my fringe from my brow.

The sensation was still fresh in my memory four months later when I stood, head bowed, by his open grave, wondering what he could see from heaven and whether he knew about the fresh black mark on my soul, the undiscovered and unpardonable sin I had committed.

"I hope it will help. You'll be normal again in no time. Now make sure your spine is straight, place your palms down flat. I will see you in the morning for breakfast."

*

When the wind is up the window of my cell rattles in its frame in such a deliberate way that I must believe it is controlled by some intelligent, external force. The pattern is repetitive, percussive. I suspect my savour is attempting to communicate with me in a language I am yet to understand. My head resting against the rubber I struggle to decipher it, without success.

More signs, more omens.

Taken out to the airing court for the first time since I scaled the wall, I am kept in my straight waistcoat and accompanied by three unspeaking men. Next to the shelter a game of quoits is taking place. Traipsing around and reinvigorating my tired legs I spot a cloud in the shape of a sow's head over where the church must stand. As I watch, it gradually transforms itself into what is what nobody could deny is the image of a barking dog.

Back in my cell cracks have appeared in the ceiling where there were no cracks before.

These portents give me the strength to wait. No longer are my days passed in a furious blur, but patiently and in peace.

*

Once a week the corset was removed to be cleaned but otherwise I wore it at all times. The end of the summer loomed, and my return to school. Would I be forced to wear it even then, in front of my peers? I could, of course, have asked my uncle whether this was to be the case but I was unprepared to make any reference to the garment, representing as it did a complete failure of character.

While it was cumbersome and uncomfortable and I worried it could be seen beneath my day clothes, I understood why it was necessary. If I was too weak willed to control my body's uglier functions then it must be done my other means. It was my sincere hope that eventually my urges would be suppressed and I would no longer need to rely on it. That longed-for victory featured heavily in my daydreams: the moment when I could shed the garment for the final time, my soul cleansed and my instincts purified.

It all seemed a very long way off. At night my thoughts were invaded by Magdalene, who taunted me with her insistent advances. I kept remembering our kiss and extending the scenario, taking it to places where in reality it did not go. I pictured her sat at the foot of my bed, her black hair hanging loose, laughing as she stroked her hand up and down my calves, mocking my resistance. At these times the tube at the front of the metal cup could be more of a hindrance than a help, becoming the cause of arousal as much as pain. The fantasy was so powerful it was a surprise to open my eyes and discover I was alone. I was thankful that the jacket prevented me from acting on my sordid impulses.

*

Seward comes in, accompanied by the Principal Attendant.

"I'm told your behaviour has been exemplary of late."

Mr Simmons nods: "He's a changed man, sir. His mania has completely subsided."

152

I get to my feet: "It's true, I have been feeling much better, Doctor Seward. I believe I am finally on the road to recovery."

"I must say I'm glad to hear it. I've had a discussion with the staff and we all agree you are ready to return to your room. I hope you realise this is an expression of trust on our part and that you will treat it accordingly."

"Of course."

"There is one condition, though. I'm concerned that you haven't been eating your meals. You occasionally eat the vegetables but reject the meat. We found the wooden box in your wardrobe, full of discarded beef and chicken. Protein is important, Renfield. You of all people should know that. Will you promise me that you'll start eating properly again?"

"I will eat whatever my body requires."

Freed from my shackles and straight waistcoat I am led through a series of broad corridors, empty but for the attendants at their gas-jets. When I am alone in my room, which had once seemed like a prison but now felt like home, I stretch my arms and roll my shoulders, slowly and methodically getting the blood flowing again. Once the sensation has returned to my fingers I use them to explore the altered contours of my face. Up until now I have had only the pressure around my eyes and cheekbones to use as a guide to how quickly I was healing after my beating.

Although I am still bruised and tender the damage is, mercifully, not as bad as I had begun to imagine. Relieved, I open the window and look out over the landscape. The church tower is nowhere to be seen.

*

Uncle Patrick was a systematic eater, finishing each individual item of food on his plate before moving on to the next: first the fried mushrooms, then the grilled tomatoes, then the egg, never mixing mouthfuls. It was a method meant to aid digestion that he encouraged me to emulate. That morning at breakfast, while he concentrated on the movements of his knife and fork, I stole a glance at his face. He had lost weight again. The skin over his cheekbones was stretched tight and thin and had developed a silvery glint. His teeth seemed too large for his mouth. The past three weeks must have left him worn-out with worry and that I was to blame seemed obvious. Sensing my gaze he looked up and I quickly lowered my head.

When I had been excused I climbed the stairs to the first floor. At the top Mrs Highsmith appeared from behind the banister and obstructed my path. "John," she whispered. She was standing too closely and I felt compelled to lean back. "John," she said again, thrusting something into my hand. "Take this." She refused to let go of my wrist until I had taken what she had given me: "Why don't you keep this in your pocket for the time being? No need for your uncle to see it, eh?"

"My name is Richard, not John."

"Of course. I'm sorry, young master Richard. Run along now."

Understanding this was to be a secret between us I went to my room and closed the door, resentful of being forced into such a position.

In my hand was a registered envelope, badly crumpled and addressed directly to me. Tearing it open I sat down and read the contents.

> DEAR RICHARD: I will be at the
> old bridge at 9 o'clock in the evening
> on Friday. I hope you find it in your
> heart to see me, if you can. I will be
> waiting.
>
> Yours, Magdalene.

I read it over three times before shoving it in my pocket and taking it down to the bottom of the garden, to a spot behind an oak tree out of sight of the house. Here, I tore it into tiny pieces and buried it in the soil.

Later that afternoon I sneaked into the kitchen and

stole a paring knife, which I smuggled into my bedroom and hid beneath the mattress.

*

In my hand I hold a Death's-head Hawkmoth. I cannot say how it came to be in my room. The sound of it tapping against the ceiling woke me from my sleep.

It flutters against my palm, making my loosely clenched fist feel independently alive, like a beating heart. Forming a narrow gap between my fingers I peak inside. The creature is fat and vibrant, its skull-shaped markings vivid on its thorax. It is not a moth but a sign. The final omen. It is time to move. Putting my hand to my mouth I tip the contents onto my tongue and bite down on the abdomen, immediately invigorated by the life blood as it flows down my throat. It is hard for me to believe I ever found the taste disgusting.

Removing my nightgown I put on my trousers, shirt and waistcoat. Once my shoes are tied I position myself against the wall behind the door and begin to wail, making noises as if I am in unbearable pain. The observation hatch snaps open.

"Renfield? What is it?" It is a new watcher, inexperienced, unsure of himself. An Irishman.

I continue to wail.

"Come out where I can see you."

"I can't. I cannot move."

"Where are you?"

"I need assistance. Please."

"Just hold on while I fetch my Mr Simmons."

"I cannot wait. I am in pain."

"All right. Give me a second."

Once he is inside I grab him around the neck and bundle him to the floor. He is a small man and easy to overcome. Covering his mouth I prize the key ring from his hand and make a dash for the door. Before I can close it fully behind me he has inserted his arm and shoulder into the gap.

"For God's sake, Renfield, please. I need this job."

We struggle and I manage to spread my hand over his face to push him back.

"I'm sorry," I say. "I wouldn't do this unless it was absolutely necessary. You'll understand eventually."

Afraid of crushing his fingers he pulls away. Even before I have turned the key in the lock he begins to bellow for help.

I will need to create a distraction if I am to succeed this time. Realising the power I hold now I am in possession of the bunch of keys I start to make my way down the corridor, opening the other doors.

"Run!" I shout. "Run! You're free!"

157

There are seven inmates in all. Two stir in their beds, dazed and half asleep, regarding me with confused expressions. A third pulls his blanket up to his chin in the manner of a frightened child, covering his hairless and sunken chest.

"I don't want to," he says. "Please don't make me."

The others leap into action and grasp the opportunity to escape, scrambling out of their rooms: the first three in their nightgowns, the fourth naked. One I recognise as the man with the constantly paint spattered hands who lights his cigarettes using the attendant's gas-jet. The room behind him is candlelit and busy with brightly coloured canvases, all depicting what appear to be pictures of cats dressed as people. The naked escapee's whole body shakes and he flashes his hands with excitement.

At the end of the corridor I use the keys to let everyone out before me. The five of us scatter in different directions. I take the stairs, running down one flight, then another, into what must be the basement. Dizzy with exhilaration I push through a set of heavy double doors and come out towards the end of what I presume is a vast service corridor, a quarter of a mile long at least, gas-lit and containing rows of laundry baskets and food trolleys. Hearing movement from the room closest to me I set off as quickly as I dare, trying to keep my footfalls as light as possible and chucking the keys into a bundle of dirty sheets. Glancing through the open doors to my sides as I go I see a succession of large empty kitchens and a silent laundry room full of industrial-scale mangles. By the time I reach the end of the corridor my old ankle injury is flaring up again. Putting it out of my mind I enter the second stairwell and pace up to the ground floor, taking three steps at a time.

Searching for a way out I come across what looks to be a long, rectangular day room with a patterned carpet runner, more cheerfully decorated than anything I have seen elsewhere in the asylum. Armchairs with embroidered antimacassars are positioned around the floor, along with tables covered by tasselled cloths and tall pot plants standing on either side of the windows. Faintly in the distance I can hear a piano being played, a melody I recognise from the distant past, from a lifetime ago: Beethoven's Piano Sonata No.14. It stops me in my tracks. The energy drains from my limbs and I am overwhelmed by a deep melancholy, a yearning for things long gone.

Through a mist of tears I see something moving beyond the open door at the other side of the room, a figure with shorn hair, wearing a loose white robe. Blinking, I see it is a woman, her skin so pale her lips have, by contrast, taken on the colour of cherries. With her head bowed and her eyes cast down she stops beneath the frame and turns in my direction. I must have inadvertently found my way into the female wards.

Afraid she might be startled by the sight of me and raise the alarm I remain perfectly still. Apparently oblivious to my presence she steps forward, her movements so languid I wonder if she might be sleepwalking. Each table she passes, each chair, she touches lightly with the tips of her fingers, as if counting them off, accompanied all the while by the sonata-allegro drifting in from another room. It is only when we are within reach of each other, roughly a yard apart, that she realises I am here with her. Stepping away she widens her eyes with fear. In a ploy to placate her I place my hand on my stomach and perform a deep, regal bow. A faltering smile spreads across her face. She is reassured. Crossing her ankles like a ballerina she responds with an elaborate curtsy and continues contentedly on her way. She is the first woman I have seen since my life in Carfax began.

Beyond this room the corridors become maze-like and complicated by mezzanines. The dividing doors, of which there are many, are made of dark varnished wood and the floors are covered with intricately patterned black, white and grey tiles. Brass plaques on the walls confirm my suspicion that I have stumbled into the administration block: ASSISTANT MEDICAL OFFICER, ENGINEER, SUPERINTENDENT. When the escape siren bursts into action, as I knew it must, I cover my ears with my hands.

Hurriedly, I double back on myself, taking the first flight of stairs I can find.

Finally: a window on the ground floor that opens when I give it a push. Swinging my legs out I lower my feet onto the grass. In the moonlight I am just able to make out the lawns ahead of me, the 'Union Jack' pathways, the trimmed hedges and the giant-like poplars which line the drive. From the direction of the main doors people are shouting. A figure in a white nightgown flashes across the space: the painter, being pursued. I must make it around to the other side of the building if I am to reach the church.

Setting off at a run I follow the grass border towards the far end of the building. After turning the corner I pass by more horticulture: Pleasure Gardens tended by the non-violent inmates, in boxes separated by gravel pathways, each with zinc plate bearing the gardener's name. Farther along, the moon is out of sight and it is considerably darker, shaded by tall firs. This time it is not necessary for me to climb the wall: there is a wooden door which takes me out onto a path across the railway line. Guessing at the direction in which I must go I start down the slope, running through trees.

When I find the low wall of the graveyard it appears so suddenly before me I almost trip over. Ahead, the church is glowing in the moonlight, its stones humming with an energy so intense I know my master and saviour must be

161

waiting within. I skip over the perimeter, avoiding a tall nettle patch, and head to the front door.

Again I am confronted by a padlock, but having more presence of mind than during my last visit I look around for a way to break it. Remembering the rusty iron gate I make my way down the stone path to test its horizontal bars and find one loose enough to remove. This I use for leverage, slipping it under the chain between the handles so I can pull against the wood. It takes all my strength but soon the brass plates are giving way, their screws coming free. Through the nearby trees the escape sirens echo back and forth. One last heave and the padlock drops.

As the door scrapes open I am greeted by the smell of mould and mildew. Nothing is visible beyond the nearest row of pews. Staring into the deep darkness I sense a powerful presence where the altar must stand. My master, at last. Putting aside my fears I plunge into the unknown, regardless of whatever obstacles might stand in my way. Twenty paces down the aisle my toes knock against a raised step. Putting my arms out I rest my hands on a slab of cold marble.

"Renfield."

The voice is soft and comforting. I hold my breath to hear it better.

"Renfield."

Realising the speaker must be somewhere behind me I

look over my shoulder. At the threshold of the open door stands a figure, silhouetted by the moonlight.

"I am here," I say.

"It is Seward, Doctor Renfield. Please don't be alarmed."

Hearing this preface triggers a flood of memories. *Doctor Renfield.* The words sound foreign to me now, distant, like the name of a character from a half-forgotten novel I read long ago. It belongs to someone else. Yet it is also my own. It is morning suits and writing bureaus. It is my leather business bag. It is my front door, my books, my excellent mind. It is pacing through the orchard at Devon County Asylum. It is the respect of others.

"Come back with me," says Seward.

Letting go of the alter I make my way down the central passageway. As I approach him the doctor's features come into focus: his boyish face, his sandy hair, the glass in his wire rimmed spectacles reflecting the moon. The youthful Medical Superintendent.

All at once I am consumed by hatred. Who is this man who seeks to prevent me from fulfilling my destiny? Who has taken my career, my position in society, my life? Here stands my replacement in all things, belittling me with his sympathy while I waste away under lock and key. But even in my diminished state I am still stronger than him. I will tear his throat out.

Charging at my enemy I leap forward take either side

163

of his head in my hands, pushing him backwards and straddling his torso. Before I can sink my teeth into him he manages to get one hand under my chin, thrusting my head away and jarring my neck. He is wide eyed, terrified. I lunge and push.

In my frenzy something catches my eye in the sky above the trees. A bat cutting a line across the moon.

As rapidly as it arrived my anger has vanished, leaving me exhausted but lucid. I step away from Seward, freeing him to search the ground for his smashed spectacles. His hair is messy, his clothes are disarranged, his cheeks are burning red. To the watchers running towards us down the stone path I raise my palms in submission then, unsteady on my feet, bend down to scoop up Seward's glasses and hand them back to him.

"You needn't tie me," I say. "I will go quietly."

PART FOUR

Seward has gone.

I learn this from the night watchers talking unhappily outside my door as they change shifts. His position is to be temporarily filled by Doctor Hennessey, dispatched from the Home Office with a reputation for being a strict disciplinarian with a brutish temper. What has become of Seward is unknown.

Reflecting on this revelation I remember an exchange Seward and I shared in my room just prior to my first escape. Fitting the wax cylinder into his phonograph he had looked weary and worn, as was so often the case in recent times. I asked him directly if he was unwell.

"I appreciate your concern but I assure you I am in very good health."

"Are you getting enough sleep?"

"No, but I'm certainly not unique in that respect these days, am I? It is the world we seem to have created for ourselves. Which brings me back to my question: do you have any theory regarding what caused your bad dreams? Did they occur more frequently when you were feeling

167

anxious, for example, or when you altered your diet?"

"There was no pattern that I can see. Also, I don't think they can accurately be described as dreams."

"What, then? Visions? Hallucinations?"

"Hallucinations, no. Visions, yes, perhaps. I would use that word only for the want of another. It implies my experiences were unreal, and I'm not at all sure that's accurate."

"Just because they occurred in your head doesn't make them any less real. Not to you, anyway."

"Sometimes I think you misunderstand deliberately, simply to vex me. What I mean, as you well know, is they were not a product of my imagination. They actually happened."

"Just as this conversation is happening now, between you and I, in this room?"

"Precisely, but on another plain, like another layer of existence, surrounding us all the time and no less solid than our own, but invisible to most. A sphere unknown."

"Why is it, do you think, you can see this different world when others cannot?"

"I have been chosen."

"Go on."

"I am being prepared."

At this point the doctor lifted his spectacles and pinched the bridge of his nose. I asked if he was sure he was feeling well.

"Perfectly well. Thank you."

If it was obvious at the time that he was being untruthful then it was even more so now, given recent events. Looking back I wonder if his complaint was emotional in its nature rather than physical, stemming from a matter of the heart. A man of his age and as yet unmarried is likely to be courting. Perhaps he is heartbroken? I can imagine the kind of woman he might fall for. Energetic, sweet-natured, somewhat naïve, like the doctor himself. It is easy to believe such a woman would attract more than one suitor. Perhaps this is the issue? Picturing her as I do I could almost fall in love with her myself.

But then, even if my speculations are true, it seems unlikely that such a state of affairs, while troubling, would be enough to take him away from his work. Therefore it must be a matter of a more serious nature. Could his beloved be ill? Again, I think of the plague, the early days of a disease destined to bring the country–the whole human race–to its knees.

I profoundly regret attacking the doctor. It was undeserved. He is a good man and means well. How could he have known that he was preventing me from finding salvation? When I think of my behaviour that night I am filled with shame. An emotion with which I am more than familiar.

*

The temporary Superintendent makes his presence known long before I meet him. Under his orders my personal effects are removed: my notebooks and pens, my daily newspaper, my books. The room appears bare without them, like a gaol again.

To this abuse I submit without protest. It is of little importance to me now. In the room next to mine the inmate has a harder time of it. When the attendants arrive *en masse* one morning to take his painting materials away he does everything he can to prevent them. On hearing his shouts I step into the corridor in time to see him wrestling with a stocky young man over a painting of a ginger cat with bright green eyes.

"I'm sorry, Mr Wainwright. I must do as I'm directed. Please let go."

"You don't know what you're doing!"

The moment the frame is tugged from his paint spattered hands the artist lets out a strangled yelp of grief and starts to cry unashamedly, a sight which embarrasses everyone present, myself included. Other attendants file out of his room and down the corridor, carrying a parade of colourful tableaux: depictions of cats in morning suits

170

out for a stroll, cats waltzing at a ball, cats on a fishing boat.

"What do you intend to do with them?" he asks in desperation.

"We're putting them into storage. They won't be damaged, I promise you."

Wainwright makes his hand into a fist and presses it against his forehead: "This is unacceptable. The Home Office will hear of it, mark my words. Shame on you."

Lastly an easel is taken from the room along with a battered box of brushes and paints. Another strangled noise bursts from my neighbour and he doubles over, sobbing with grief. Stepping into my room I push the door closed.

When Hennessey finally visits he is accompanied by a subdued looking Mr Simmons, to whom he addresses all his comments. I observe him from the edge of my bed.

"So, this is Seward's pet, the famous Mr Renfield, the 'zoophagous maniac'. Let me see."

From under one of his meaty arms he produces a folder of notes, adjusting his pince-nez to consult them. His mouth is hidden by a great moustache, a different shade of brown to the wig that balances unconvincingly on his scalp. I observe his medicine-ball paunch with disapproval.

In his irritatingly nasal voice he reads from the front page: "R. M. Renfield, age fifty-nine. Sanguine temperament, great physical strength, periods of gloom, ending in some fixed idea which I cannot make out... possibly dangerous..." Impatiently, he flips the sheet over. "Then more balderdash. I've encountered his kind many times before. A hopeless case, if ever I've seen one. It will be a long time until he can be considered sane again, if it ever happens at all." The statement is punctuated by a luxuriantly phlegmatic cough. "Right, on to the next one."

He exits without having so much as glanced in my direction, as if I am not present at all. It gives me some idea of what it must feel like to be a ghost, an inhabitant of a secondary plane: invisible, unconsidered.

I am fifty-nine. An old man. This I did not know.

*

This vision is different. I am not a participant but an observer of events occurring far away. I am there but not there. As if I am looking through a telescope.

Here is a hallway, lined with bouquets of flowers. Walking its length is a woman of transfixing beauty in a loose white nightdress, gently brushing the rose petals as she goes by. Her skin is pale, her hair blonde. She seems familiar to me, but not intimately so. At first I wonder if it is the woman who accompanied Elise on the night before I began my vigil but then, instinctively, I know better. It is the woman Seward has fallen in love with. Her name is Lucy.

Only when she reaches the end of the corridor and comes to the top of a flight of stairs do I notice her eyes are closed, as if she is sleepwalking or under some kind of spell. Terrified she will fall I reach out to hold her back. Then I remember I am in a different place and unable to intervene. When she begins to descend I am hugely relieved: her steps are assured and well-placed. She knows this route well. This must be her home. Without faltering she floats down two flights to the ground floor.

The front door opens and we are looking out over a coastal town, built around a river running through a deep valley that opens into a harbour. Out of the small front garden Lucy goes, then down a hill, passing rows of pastel coloured cottages. The full moon appears from behind a cloud and lights up the sea.

The streets of the old town are silent as she moves through them and works her way towards the bay. Passing a wattle and daub public house with a painting of a black swan on its sign, she reaches the waterside. Moored boats creak against their hawsers, waves slap against the harbour side. From here she crosses a wooden swing bridge and heads away from the piers, finally joining a coastal path that will take her up to the hill overlooking the town. Has nobody noticed she is missing from her home? Where is

Seward?

As she climbs, the hem of her nightdress drags along the dirt. The unsheltered track is winding and steep in places but she follows it without hesitation, as confidently as she tackled the stairs, as if her eyes are open and it is middle of the day. Still, she has come perilously close to where the land falls away. One slip would send her tumbling to the rocks below. Another young life ended in its prime.

Not again. Not again.

At the edge of the cliff she hesitates, her head bowed and her hair caught in the light breeze, then turns and joins a sandy path leading to the ruins of an abbey. From here there is a view all the way up to the headland where a granite wall stretches out into the water, running parallel to a sturdy black sea wall. A buoy with a bell rings out slowly, mournfully.

Beyond the abbey is a parish church rounded by a graveyard, where Lucy's journey ends. Taking a bench next to the point at which the land drops–so dramatically that some of the bank has collapsed, leaving dozens of tombstones projecting over the cliff–she sits down and places her hands over her lap. As she rests I realise I have been given a rare opportunity. Without fear of being discovered I can study her delicate features, her milky skin, and the pale hairs on her arms. A shadow falls across the graveyard as the moon slips behind clouds.

Lucy's position is changing, so gradually that at first it is almost undetectable. Her muscles are relaxing, her posture becoming less rigid. Eventually her hands part and fall to her sides. Her head drops back. It is as if the life is being drained from her body.

Something dark is shifting in the shadows behind the bench, a palpable presence that refuses to hold its shape. Now it resembles a great bird, now a bear, now a sooty-black animal like a monstrous cat. Lucy slumps and slips forward in the seat, her legs pushed wide apart. The cat swells into a great palpitating mass.

"Get away!"

It turns in my direction. It senses me: it heard my shout. Sending me a warning it bristles and hisses, arching its back. Its eyes are cold and depthless black. I have seen them before.

Then, all at once, it is gone.

*

When the young Irish attendant arrives with my porridge I ask him to pass a message to Doctor Hennessey. I must speak with him again as a matter of urgency. It is my intention to demand my immediate release.

Since the vision I have been unable to rest. I am

constantly anxious, my stomach is unsettled. If what I witnessed is to be believed—and I see no reason why it should not—then it is clear I have been deceived and betrayed. No doubt my master selected me because I was at my lowest ebb and vulnerable to manipulation. Using promises of protection and rebirth he sought to utilize me as a pawn in his game, the end purpose of which he intended to conceal until the last moment. This is why he sent such obscure clues and ambiguous signs: to baffle me and distract me from the truth.

He is a parasite. He is preying on Lucy to build his own strength and he hopes to use me to gain access to further victims. He wants me to let him inside the asylum.

With Lucy's lifeblood being incrementally drained she cannot survive for much longer. It is my duty as a human being to find her and save her, whatever it takes. Perhaps, in doing so, I will be able to atone for the sins of my past and be granted deliverance.

*

Waiting for an audience with the new Superintendent is almost intolerable. Every time an attendant or a watcher passes by I reassert my request in the strongest possible terms, but still Hennessey stays away. If only he understood what is at stake. I am beside myself thinking of poor Lucy, wasting away, vulnerable and defenceless against this super-natural force. Soon it will be too late and the creature will have drained her last drop of life. However frustrated I feel, though, I must control my anger. I can only hope that my messages are being conveyed accurately; that they are being related at all.

My frantic suffering comes to an end when I finally hear his high pitched voice approaching from the end of the corridor, delivering abrupt instructions to Mr Simmons. Rushing to make myself presentable I straighten my clothes and compose my expression. He must leave me convinced of my sanity. To improve my posture I imagine a length of string attached to the top of my head, pulling me upwards: a trick taught to me by my uncle.

He enters and I offer my hand to shake, but he declines to take it.

"Sir," I say. "Thank you for making the time to see me. I appreciate you must be extremely busy. I trust you are well?"

He stays near the door, casting his narrow eyes over the room to see it has been cleared of my home comforts as he ordered: "What do you want?"

"I see my messages have not reached you. Very well. At least you are here now." For a horrific moment I realise I have neglected to comb my hair. Hurriedly I lick my palm and run it over my fringe before continuing. "Had the attendants done as they were asked"-I throw an accusatory glance at Simmons-"you would know I wish to discuss the possibility of my parole. As you will be aware from Doctor Seward's notes I have experienced some problems with my temper in the past but I can assure you that, firstly, I only ever reacted in the face of the severest provocation and, secondly, I now have everything under control. I am quite back to my old self, due no doubt in part to the excellent treatment provided by this fine establishment."

Hennessey removes his pince-nez and methodically cleans the lenses with a cloth: "Yes, well, I'm afraid that isn't going to be possible."

"Are you not even going to make a proper evaluation? I can assure you, doctor, I am perfectly sane. Surely a man of your experience can see that at a glance?"

"Mr Renfield. Your mood is by turns melancholic and maniacal. You are prone to violence. You have shown an unhealthy obsession with eating insects. I cannot risk allowing you back into society."

Needing a moment to think I lift my heels and place them down again: "Perhaps if I explained myself."

"There really is no need. Good-day to you."

Seeing he is about to leave I have no choice but to raise my voice: "Lives are at stake, sir!"

He hesitates: "And why might that be?"

"Doctor Seward. He is away with an acquaintance of

178

his, no? On the coast?"

"His current whereabouts are none of your concern. His is not your friend, Renfield, no matter how he presents himself to his prisoners."

"I don't need you to confirm it. I have seen it with my own eyes and know it to be the truth. I also know the name of his acquaintance to be Lucy and that she is in mortal danger."

I have succeeded in piquing his interest, at least, although his hand still rests on the door handle: "How so?"

"Are you familiar with the practice of soul murder?"

"I am not."

"There is no reason why you should be. The concept is not widely known. I have only recently stumbled across it myself, through my observation of spiders and flies. Not an 'unhealthy obsession', you see, but a scientific study."

"Go on."

"Firstly allow me to explain the true nature of the soul. The place it holds in the natural world is unique, it being neither material nor immaterial, as incorporeal as it is earthly. In humans it is located at the back of the skull, around the base of the tongue. For the most part it is undetectable to its owner: only those with an extremely vigorous soul can sense its presence. Even I, for many years, was ignorant of it, even privately doubted its existence, until it became impossible to deny. The powerful soul, you see, betrays itself with a constant pressure at the back of the head, against the skull wall, which can be the cause of sleeplessness and distorted vision. Dreams become remarkably vivid as the body enters a state of near unending excitedness."

I am speaking too quickly and in danger of confusing my audience. I wet my lips, steady my breathing and try to slow down.

"As blood passes through the back of the head and the throat it acquires some of the soul's vitality, which it transports to the body's extremities. In this way the owner is kept alive. Natural death occurs when the soul escapes, rises into the air and disperses; an act which the owner of a vibrant soul can actually perceive. Without its nourishment blood becomes mere matter, lifeless. What I have now learned is that it is possible to take possession of another person's soul: poets and storytellers have known this for centuries, of course. This cannot be achieved quickly. The soul cannot be removed instantaneously from its source. Instead it must be passed gradually, through the intermediary of blood. The blood can be extracted from any part of the body and fed directly into one's own, through the mouth or by other means, but it is especially potent when taken directly from around the throat, where it has only recently flowed through the soul's centre. The extraction of the blood puts the body's vitality at risk, causing the soul to release more of itself in order to replenish the stream. This process takes roughly twenty-four hours. If blood is drawn from the body with enough frequency the soul will eventually become entirely depleted. With no source of replenishment the body dies, while the person who has taken possession of the soul finds their own is strengthened, and their life prolonged. In this way it is possible to achieve immortality."

Unburdening myself is exhilarating and exhausting. My hands are trembling.

"This is what is happening to Seward's friend. Some time ago now, I cannot say when, I fell under the influence of a very powerful being, someone who I suspect used to be human but has since evolved into something new, something greater. It is my belief that he has been committing soul murder for centuries, keeping himself alive by drawing on the strength of others. I do not know his name or from where he comes. All I can say is that for a while I wanted nothing more than to serve and assist him, tempted by his promises of salvation, but now I have seen his true nature my conscience will not allow it. Every night he visits Lucy, entrancing her and sipping away at her soul, sucking the blood through her skin like a leech. The people around her, no doubt, believe her to be anaemic. Soon she will have no more life left to give. Only I have communicated directly with the perpetrator. Only I can find a way to stop him. Therefore I urge you, for the sake of this young woman, for the sake of Seward, you must let me go."

With the sweat cooling on my forehead I wait for Hennessey's response.

He strokes his chin: "Remarkable. I can see why Seward became so fascinated by your case. However, it is abundantly clear you are lost in some elaborate fantasy and becoming progressively more so. There is no way I can sanction your parole."

Disregarding my calls he leaves and makes his way down the corridor, with Simmons at his heels: "You must believe me," I shout. "This cannot be allowed to happen. Doctor!"

But it is useless. He is gone.

*

An attendant arrives to tell me I have a visitor.

"A visitor? Are you certain?"

"Of course I'm certain. Come along now. We don't want to keep the gentleman waiting."

After putting on my frock coat I am led to a day room on the ground floor, which looks more like a working men's club than anything you might expect to find in Carfax, cluttered with tables for reading and chequered boards for draughts and chess. Stood alone by a large bay window and removing his Inverness tweed cape is my old friend David Toynbee.

"Richard," he says by way of greeting.

He has aged: the lines around his face have deepened, his face has fallen slightly. Shaken by his unexpected arrival I flounder, standing in the doorway and unsure how to respond.

"Won't you come in?"

"Of course, please take a chair," I say, as if welcoming a guest into my home rather than a visitor into a madhouse.

"I'm sorry I haven't come before now. It is good to see you."

Waiting in silence while the attendant brings a tray of Dundee cake and tea, I notice my friend is wearing an expensive looking gold and bloodstone ring. My hands are shaking.

"How have you been?" he says.

"Fine. As well as can be expected. How did you get here?"

"By rail."

I am finding it difficult to maintain my composure. My heart is thumping in my chest and I am overly conscious of the way I am sitting. We face each other across the table just as we might have during one of our evenings in Marylebone, but the balance has shifted. Once we were

183

equals.

"I'm not here only to see you, although I have been looking forward to it, of course. I've come on official business." He meets my eyes for the first time since I arrived, gauging my reaction. "I'm a Visitor in Lunacy now."

I cross and uncross my legs.

He continues: "Hollings retired and I was offered the post last year. It came as something of a surprise but I was happy to accept it. I had been starting to make preparations to move the family to New York but it was an opportunity I didn't feel I could let pass. As you can imagine, I have been kept busy. This is my first trip to Carfax."

Still unable to find the right words I look out across the autumnal lawns, where orange and red leaves shaken from the tall poplars scatter cross the gravel paths. My companion taps his foot up and down in the air. After a while he asks if I am being well treated.

"I have had my personal effects removed."

"I'm sorry to hear that. Do you want me to have a word with Hennessey? He'll listen to me, I'm sure. I won't give him a choice, the old fool."

"That won't be necessary.... When was the last time we met, do you suppose? It is difficult to keep track of time in here."

"I'm not sure. I assume I came for an evening visit to

your home. It couldn't have been long after I came back from America."

There is another prolonged pause.

"My family are doing well," he continues. "Andrew is flourishing at university. Marie wasn't well pleased at my new appointment, of course, seeing how frequently it takes me away from home, but she became accustomed to it soon enough. I rather suspect she prefers it when I'm gone."

"And how are things at the Commission?"

"That's something I wanted to discuss with you, actually. It looks very much like Henry Drinkwater is about to be selected as the Secretary. What do you make of that?"

I am shocked he would ask me: "I am in no position to comment. Surely you know that."

"Please, Richard, you know I always trusted you on such matters."

"He may have changed completely, for all I know. I've had no contact from anybody at the Commission since I came here. None at all."

"I can assure you, he has not changed in the least. Still the same old stubborn mule. Still pontificating."

"In which case I would say the suggestion is startlingly idiotic. The man has never displayed any understanding whatsoever of life in a madhouse. Besides which he insists on expressing himself like he's speaking from pulpit rather

185

than in the proper language of a doctor. It is infuriating. He is a buffoon."

David nods: "Yes, that was my assessment too. Thank you. It's always good to have your own opinions reinforced."

We speak for a while about further changes at the Home Office, the progress of my old acquaintances. The Evangelical clique, I am glad to hear, have begun to lose their influence. Then, just as I am beginning to relax and enjoy the company of my friend, it is time for him to go, leaving me with promises of another visit as soon as his schedule allows. Returning to my room I am elated. He cannot know how transforming it is to have my opinion sought and valued, to feel useful in some small way. Even the four walls around me seem altered, as if I am perceiving them through new eyes. For a while it is possible to think of myself as Doctor Renfield, ex-Superintendent of Devon County Asylum and an admired Visitor in Lunacy, rather than an outcast, an imprisoned lunatic.

The rest of the day I spend in rumination. In this new attitude I find myself questioning for the first time whether I am as rational as I believed. Had someone challenged my view of the world only a few hours earlier I would have directed them to the evidence: the miraculous gift of the sparrow, the church conjured from air, the Death's-head Hawkmoth. But now I find myself re-evaluating.

I stare through my window, out over the empty landscape. Something moves in slowly from the left of the scene. A farmer working with a horse-driven plough. There is no great plague. Beyond these walls life continues as it always has.

Could I, in the grip of a delusion, have misinterpreted everything? Is a bat nothing more than a bat?

*

When Seward returns I am reluctant to ask where he has been. My thinking has been so clear recently I am worried his answer might upset me and disturb the balance. I have been sleeping regularly for the past few weeks, free from visions or hallucinations. Although it takes a feat of concentration I am mostly able to keep my more troubling thoughts pushed to the back of my mind. If I have been sick then I am recovering.

The Superintendent looks in good health. When he arrives in my room it is clear he has just come from the grounds: his hair is tousled from the wind and his cheeks are flushed. On saying hello he passes me a newspaper, presumably aware Hennessey put a stop to my daily delivery. No mention is made of our last encounter, when I behaved so unforgivably. It is as if it never happened.

"How are you, Renfield? You look well. You've gained a little weight around the face."

"I have been feeling a great deal more settled."

"I'm very glad to hear it. Look, I hope you don't mind but I have brought someone who would like to meet you."

I am startled: "Another visitor? Waiting outside?"

"A good friend of mine, come to see where I spend my days."

My last meeting with someone from the outside world did so much to improve my spirits I am barely able to conceal my enthusiasm: "Very well. Let them come in, by all means, but just wait a minute while I tidy the place."

Seward stands by patiently as I tuck my bed sheets and straighten what few possessions I have left. When I am ready I sit myself down on the edge of the bed, crossing my legs and leaving the chair free for my guest.

"Please, show them in."

The doctor steps into the corridor and returns followed by a black haired woman in a white dress. My breath catches.

It is Magdalene.

She offers her hand. I stand and accept it while she performs a shallow bow. She is a grown woman now but it as if she has barely aged at all: her complexion is rich and brilliant, her features small and beautifully formed: "Good evening, Mr Renfield. You see, I know you, for Doctor Seward has told me of you."

The Superintendent introduces my guest as Mrs Harker.

I release her hand, realising I have been holding it for too long: "Delighted to meet you."

"I am sorry not to have given more warning of my visit. We seem to have given you a shock."

"Not at all. You are very welcome. Please, sit. Mrs Harker, yes?"

"That's right."

I cannot tear my eyes from her face. If she is not Magdalene after all then her resemblance to my childhood friend is uncanny. Momentarily I entertain the notion that she might have changed her name and forgotten who I am.

"So how long have you been here for, Mr Renfield?"

I am still trying to work out who she might be: "You're not the girl the doctor wanted to marry, are you? You can't be, you know, for she must be dead by now."

A hesitant sideways glance at Seward is followed by a smile: "Oh no, I have a husband of my own, to whom I was married before I ever saw Doctor Seward, or he me. Mr Harker has come to help your Superintendent with some work and I have accompanied him."

"How did you know I wanted to marry anyone?" Seward, I see, has been regarding me quizzically.

189

I splutter: "What an asinine question."

Mrs Harker jumps to her friend's defence: "I don't see that at all, Mr Renfield."

Wishing to ingratiate myself with this sweet lady I quickly change my tone: "You will, of course, understand, Mrs Harker, that when a man is so loved and honoured as our host is, everything regarding him becomes of interest in our little community. Doctor Seward is loved not only by his household and his friends, but even by his patients, who, being some of them hardly in mental equilibrium, are apt to distort causes and effects."

My little speech pleases me. Something of my old voice is returning.

Mrs Harker turns to the doctor: "Your Mr Renfield is not at all as I imagined, John."

We continue to talk for some time. She tells me of her experiences as a schoolmistress and how she has been practising shorthand in the hope of assisting her husband in his work as a solicitor. I, in turn, allude to my past lives as a Superintendent and a member of the Lunacy Commission. None of this appears to surprise her. It seems Seward has already done a thorough job of detailing my fall from grace.

She asks, also, about my interest in spiders and flies, bringing the matter up none-too-subtly. The subject clearly intrigues her and I am happy to have the chance to disassociate myself from some of my former ideas.

"I used to fancy that life was a positive and perpetual entity, and that by consuming a multitude of live things, no matter how low in the scale of creation, one might indefinitely prolong one's own existence: relying of course, upon the Scriptural phrase, 'For the blood is the life.' Though, indeed, the vendor of a certain nostrum has vulgarized the truism to the very point of contempt. Isn't that true, doctor? I am much recovered now. The delusion is fading and I am lucid once again."

"It pleases me to hear it, Mr Renfield."

Seward is unconvinced. He thinks I have some ulterior motive and this is all a part of my greater plan. He makes a show of checking his pocket watch: "We should go. Van Helsing will be waiting for us at the station."

"Very well," says Mrs Harker, then, turning her dark and lustrous eyes towards me: "Goodbye, and I hope I may see you often, under auspices pleasanter to yourself."

Again I stand and take her hand, even though she did not offer it: "Goodbye, my dear."

After they have gone I am presented with a plate of food, my afternoon meal of carrots, boiled potatoes and beef. Sitting on the foot of my bed I pull my chair towards me to use as a table. The carrots are eaten first, then the potatoes, and finally the meat. Not long ago I would have pushed the meat to one side, rejecting the lifeless flesh as disgusting and lacking in sustenance. Chewing it thoroughly I allow myself to become reacquainted with the taste. Once the last piece has been swallowed–the only full meal I have eaten for as long as I can remember–I lay the cutlery neatly side by side.

*

For the first time since my incarceration I go to another room along the corridor and knock on the door. As I wait for a response the Irish attendant at his gas jet raises his hand to me in greeting and I do the same in reply.

"Hold on a moment," comes a voice from within. When Mr Wainwright opens the door he is wiping his paint-spattered hands with a cloth. "Oh. It's you."

I introduce myself as Richard: "And you are Mr Wainwright, is that correct? May I come in?"

After checking over his shoulder he smiles beneath his carefully cultivated moustache then steps to the side: "Yes, please do."

If his room is the same size as my own then it doesn't appear so, crammed as it is with canvases. Every inch of hanging space is occupied and stacks of paintings, five or six deep, lean against the walls. In the centre is an easel covered by a sheet, next to which stands a small table where he has rested his cigar. Clearly Seward arranged for his things to be removed from storage. As he organises a place for me to sit we go over the details of the night of our escape. He was chased around the lawns for over an hour, he tells me, spending ten minutes amongst the branches of a tall tree before finally being apprehended.

"So, what brings you all the way over here to see me?"

I hesitate, having momentarily failed to understand that he is making a joke concerning the short distance between his room and my own: "I wondered if you'd be kind enough to show me your paintings? I saw them fleetingly when Hennessey was having his clear out and now they've been returned I wanted to have a proper look."

In truth, I have decided that it would be nice to make a friend here, and expressing an interest in his art work seems like a reasonable way to strike up a conversation.

"I'm afraid I'm sure they're of no interest to anyone but me. But you're welcome to have a look around. All I'd say is, please, don't touch them."

On closer inspection the collection reveals itself to have a clear order. The paintings occupying the left hand side of the room are comical in style, like illustrations for children's books. The felines stand on their hind legs, engaging in everyday human activities. One depicts a cat in a nightgown holding a candlestick, getting ready for bed. Another has a tabby sitting on a train hiding behind a newspaper while an elderly, grey haired cat sits opposite.

At the front of a stack leaning against the wall is one that particularly catches my eye: a tom in a morning suit taking a stroll in a park, tipping his hat towards what appears to be a molly pushing a pram, although she is half concealed by a rose bush.

Following the paintings to the right reveals a gradual change in style. Landscapes are replaced by full face, head and shoulder portraits and the subjects lose their clothes. Their eyes become unnaturally wide and the pallet expands to include greens, reds and purples. Beyond the midpoint of the room they have come to barely resemble animals at all, their fur having expanded like an explosion to fill the whole canvas, a blast of colours: part cat, part Catherine wheel.

"Are these arranged in the order they were painted?"

"Roughly, I suppose. Not by design. It just seems to have happened that way."

"Have you never thought of selling them? They are excellent."

I detect a crack in his amiable and relaxed exterior: "No," he says, taking a brush to clean as something to occupy his hands. "No, I could never do that. They are too much a part of me."

"I understand. There's no reason why you should. May I see what you're working on currently?"

He is somewhat reluctant, I can tell, but the

compulsion to be friendly encourages him to remove the sheet. Beneath is a work-in-progress that shows another clear break in style. Gone are the vivid colours of his recent creations, replaced by muddy browns and dull reds. In some ways the picture bears more resemblance to his earlier works and features two cartoon-like cats up on their hind legs, side by side. One figure is a sketch in pencil, yet to be filled in. It wears a blank expression and stares directly out at the viewer. The other is painted in full, with spiky grey fur and large black eyes. Unique amongst all Mr Wainwright's creations it is baring its fangs, hissing angrily at something to its side, beyond the confines of the frame.

I ask where he draws his inspiration from. Do the pictures represent scenes from stories he has read? Why is he so fascinated by cats?

He shrugs: "I have given that a great deal of thought. I really have no idea. You don't choose your subjects, I suspect. It's more as if they choose you."

"And this fellow here, up on his claws: what is he hissing at?"

He takes a moment to ponder: "A threat of some sort. A malignancy."

*

Under the roof of the shelter, tucked between two

195

beams, a sack of eggs rests behind a delicate but dense web. The airing court is unusually peaceful, populated by a single attendant and two men sitting together beside the outer wall, conversing with such civility it is possible to imagine we are passing the afternoon in an autumnal public park rather than in the grounds of an asylum. Resting against the bench I look around for the mother spider but she is nowhere to be seen.

In the spider's nest I detect no symbolism, no oblique messages. Only life going blandly about the business of a reproducing itself. It suddenly occurs to me that my past preoccupations have not troubled me all morning. I no longer even need to make an effort to keep them from my mind. I take a lungful of fresh air. I am not the same man I was before: I am not Doctor Renfield the metropolitan physician, the Visitor in Lunacy with his business bag and his expensive suits. I am merely Renfield, resident of Carfax, friend of Craig Wainwright.

The flooring behind me creaks. Turning to see who might be approaching I am shocked to see Hardy, dressed not in an attendant's uniform but scruffy trousers and a shirt turned up at the sleeves.

"I bet you thought you'd never see me again."

There is violence concealed in the way he holds himself: his head is thrust forward and his shoulders are tense. His face is ruddy and his eyes bulging more than ever. There is dirt on his hands, packed under his fingernails. I check my surroundings and remind him that one of his colleagues stands nearby and another is bound to come along soon.

"You think I'm stupid, don't you? You might consider yourself cleverer than me but don't forget, you're nothing but a filthy, common criminal. A lunatic. I'm not half as dumb as you think, not even close to it. I wouldn't do anything to you here in broad daylight. I'll be patient, bide my time."

"I have no ill will towards you. I don't blame you for beating me. We are all a slave to our baser urges from time to time."

"I don't care what you think of me. I'm not so forgiving. Because of you Seward has me working in the gardens, on my hands and knees in the mud. My back aches all the time. My wages were cut."

"None of that was my decision."

"He should have let me kill you, you know? Who would care? One less drooling idiot in the world. They should put the lot of you to death, save us all the trouble." He sniffs and runs the back of his hand under his nose. "Don't think that just because I'm not an attendant any more I can't get around the building as I please. I've still got friends here. I've still got access to keys. If you get my meaning."

He comes close, looking deep into my eyes. I am afraid

of him but I refuse to turn away. A breeze passes through the shelter, carrying the smell of his sweat towards me.

"I will call for help if you don't step back."

"See this face?" he mutters. "Remember it. Because it's going to be the last thing you see on this Earth."

When he has gone I sit down on the bench and wait for my legs to stop shaking.

*

Drifting into sleep I think nothing at first of the sound of barking. It is only when I remember I have never once heard or seen a dog in the vicinity of Carfax that I am shocked into wakefulness, beset by images of the drooling beast at my throat on Marylebone Road.

It is crucial that I keep irrational thoughts away. The hour is late, I tell myself. You are in a dream state, only half awake. There is nothing to fear. Still, my heart races in my chest.

The window shutter judders in its frame. My eyes should have grown accustomed to the darkness, but instead the room appears to be growing incrementally blacker, as if a shadow is creeping across it: dirty water seeping into paper. An optical illusion bought on by tiredness, surely.

Getting out of bed I search for something to jam into

the side of the frame in the hope of silencing the rattle. Away from the protection of my blanket I feel cold and exposed. A shiver passes over me. Finding the newspaper given to me by Seward resting on my bedside table, I tear a strip from the front page and fold it into a wedge, but find I have made it too thick. Tearing off a smaller strip, I try again.

A noise comes from the other side of the window. A series of clicks, three of them, like finger snaps. I hold my breath. Stepping slowly away I wonder whether I should call for the night watcher but remind myself I am weary, and therefore prone to hallucination. There is no rational reason to raise the alarm, and I am a rational man. All I need do to reassure myself is look outside.

Lifting the latch I pull the shutter open, and there he is. Not a ghost or a phantom, neither a man or a beast, neither living or dead but all things mingled, a solid body, floating a storey from the ground, the palms of his hands pressed against the glass. He is younger than when we last met, the moustache which was once grey and thin is now full and black. His dark grey suit is pristine and his skin is smooth: where he once had wrinkles his flesh is plump and shining with health. Some ten feet below a heavy fog hangs, dense enough to block out the land. Losing my footing I fall backwards to the floor, dropping the newspaper at my side. My master is angry, impatient, bearing teeth as sharp as a cat's. An acrid smelling hotness spreads over my crotch and thighs.

With the forefinger of his left hand he taps the glass. He wishes me to invite him in. I look towards the door to the corridor but he only shakes his head: do not call for help, he is telling me. You will not live to regret it.

Again he taps the glass, triggering in the pit of my belly a deep physical yearning I recognise from many years before, a strange tumultuous excitement, pleasure mingled with a sense of fear and disgust. I am conscious of desire but also abhorrence. If I am to avoid repeating the sins of my past I must resist. I struggle to my feet, wondering how I must appear to him: a violently trembling wretch in a piss-sodden gown. Looking down I realise I am tumescent and use my hands to cover myself.

He speaks, but without words. You have betrayed me. You have been untrusting, ungrateful and impatient. I should crush you for this. But I am merciful. If you invite me inside I will put an end to your suffering.

In response I shake my head. He fixes me with his eyes — black like sea-polished stones — and suddenly I am somewhere else. He is showing me something, placing a vision in my head of events occurring far away.

We are in Lambeth Marsh, in the area surrounding what I recognise as Belvedere Road, amongst the tenant shacks and warehouses. A ripe stink of hops and yeast pervades the place, leaking from the nearby brewery. Moving slowly and noiselessly through the shadows is a woman, her long white hair hanging over her shallow-cheeked and silvery face. It is Lucy, but somehow altered. If there is a purpose to her journey then I cannot fathom it.

Soon she happens across a girl of eight or ten-years-old standing on a street corner. On seeing this strange woman approach the girl looks afraid, but is reassured when Lucy places a hand softly on her shoulder and proposes something that I cannot quite hear. Together they drift up the sloping, uneven pavement. There are tanning yards here, and blacking factories and lime-burners, their huge doors closed for the night. Anyone passing through at this time does so with questionable motives.

The pair turns a corner into a narrow alley between distained wooden fences. The little girl seems quite taken by her new companion, with her unblemished skin and her flowing gown. Farther away from the road they go, into the darkness. Finally Lucy takes the girl by the shoulders and turns her body to face her then, with one hand, unfastens her grubby collar and pulls the material loose. Seeing her neck is dirty she licks her fingers and wipes it clean. The girl submits and smiles uncertainly. When Lucy bends down and puts her mouth to her throat she flinches but does not pull away.

A whistle blows. Down the alley lumbers a policeman, curious at what manner of transaction is taking place. Catching sight of him Lucy turns and flees, disappearing down an adjacent track and leaving her victim to fall first to her knees then heavily onto her front. The policeman is about to make chase when he spots blood pooling onto the pathway, gushing forcefully from the little girl's neck. Blowing his whistle again he calls out for help, fumbling to stem the flow with his fingers, but it does no good. She will not survive.

In an instant I am back in my room. Rushing angrily forward I slam the shutter and fasten the latch. There are no more taps or clicks, no sounds at all. Gradually the powerful smell of rotting vegetation that had overtaken the room fades, as does my physical shame.

So this is what has become of Seward's beloved and perhaps is coming to us all. Lucy has died but lived on, condemned to an existence obeying a thirst that can never be quenched, replenishing the lifeblood stolen from her by her own murderer. She is no longer a human but an animal, condemning her prey to the same fate. Talk of an imminent plague has not been unfounded after all.

*

At one time in my life this would have been a jury of

peers. Four men of science stand in my room, two of whom I have encountered before.

"I demand to be discharged," I say, "with immediate effect."

Seward had been conducting a group tour of his facility when I asked for him to be fetched as a matter of urgency. I imagine it is only because he happened to be passing directly through my ward that he consented so quickly. In his company – introduced one by one by the Superintendent - are Doctor Godalming from Sutton Asylum, Professor Van Helsing, Mr Quincey Morris, and Mr Jonathan Harker.

Seward pushes his spectacles up the bridge of his nose: "I see. You have already discussed this matter with Doctor Hennessey, have you not?"

"Yes, but my situation has altered. It has become more important than ever that my request is granted. And you- with respect to the man who acted as your replacement-are not Doctor Hennessey." Feeling confident of my capability to make a convincing case I address the whole room. "I also appeal to your friends. They will, perhaps, not mind sitting in judgement on me?"

"I am very busy at the moment. Let's save this for another time, shall we?"

Brushing this aside I reach out my arm and greet Doctor Godalming: "Sir, we have met before, although I would understand if you do not recognise me at once. It was many years ago and my circumstances have altered somewhat in the meantime. I am Doctor Richard Renfield."

His clear embarrassment at the assertion that we might already be acquainted is quickly followed by a glint of recognition which opens the way to a burst of ill-concealed astonishment. The blood rushes to his jug-handle ears.

"Yes," he says, reluctantly shaking my hand and forcing his flat lips into a hesitant smile: "Of course. I believe I do remember you. Forgive me, I had no idea you were here."

"I am pleased to see you again after all this time. And Mr Morris," - the American has been smiling to himself but now his luxuriant moustache turns sharply down at the ends - "from hearing your accent as you came down the corridor I assume you are a Texan. You should be proud of your great State. Its reception into the Union was a precedent which may have far reaching effects hereafter, when the Pole and the Tropic may hold allegiance to the Stars and Stripes."

With little choice but to follow Godalming's lead in these peculiar circumstances, Mr Morris also accepts my outstretched hand and tips his hat: "You two know each other?"

"From a very, very long time ago," says Godalming, before I have a chance to reply. "He used to work for the

204

Lunacy Commission."

Morris raises a bushy eyebrow: "The Lunacy Commission? Well. I believe that's what you might call *irony.*"

I turn to the next person in the row, Mr Jonathan Harker. Taking his hand in both my own I tell him I had the great pleasure of meeting Mrs Harker only yesterday.

"She mentioned it to me," he replies. He is a handsome man, tall and strong-shouldered with a low hairline and an elegant profile.

"Your wife is a wonderful woman of great beauty, intelligence and sympathy. It stands to reason that her husband must be a similarly remarkable human being."

"It is very kind of you to presume as much. She was highly complementary about you also."

Pausing to let this sink in I squeeze his hand again: "Thank you. Thank you so much. You can't know how much it means to hear it."

"Are we nearly done here, Renfield?" says Seward.

Worried I shall become overwhelmed with emotion at Mr Harker's kindness I quickly transfer my attention to my final guest, who stands with his arms across his chest and his brows furrowed: "And what shall any man say at the pleasure of meeting Van Helsing? *Mijnheer, u bent een bron van inspiratie.*"

I had recognised his name, of course, when Seward

205

mentioned it the other day. The Dutchman is much admired amongst scientific circles and beyond, famous across most of Europe as an advanced medical man, a philosopher and a metaphyicist. I even wrote a series of essays about him when I was editor of *The Mind*. Given his reputation it seems fitting that his physical stature is imposing. He is solidly built with a hard, square chin and reddish hair that falls naturally back from his large forehead. As I speak he fixes me with his wide set, serious eyes.

"Sir, I make no apology for dropping all forms of conventional prefix. When an individual has revolutionized therapeutics by his discovery of the continuous evolution of brain matter, conventional forms are unfitting, since they would seem to limit him to one of a class. *Dit is een eer.* I understand our own Doctor Seward was once a pupil of yours, is that correct?"

"You are a patient here?"

"Yes. Yes, I am."

"A criminal."

This blunt statement wrong-foots me and steals the moisture from my mouth: "I suffered a severe disturbance of my cerebral function. I was not myself."

His expression betrays no reaction, no judgement. He merely completes the exchange by releasing my hand.

Endeavouring to regain the appearance of composure I

address myself to the group: "You, gentlemen, who by nationality, by heredity, or by the possession of natural gifts, are fitted to hold your respective places in the moving world, I take to witness that I am as sane as at least the majority of men who are in full possession of their liberties. And I am sure that you, Doctor Seward, humanitarian and medico-jurist as well as scientist, will deem it a moral duty to deal with me as one to be considered as under exceptional circumstances."

Seward folds his arms: "That you are improving rapidly is in no doubt, and it may well be the case that your sanity has been restored, but I cannot make such a decision without giving it serious thought and consideration first. As you can tell, I have a lot to attend to at the moment, so I suggest I will come for a longer discussion with you in the morning, after which time I will see what I can do in the direction of meeting his wishes."

"But I fear, Doctor Seward, that you hardly apprehend my wish. I desire to go at once, here, now, this very hour, this very moment." Scrutinizing the faces of these distinguished men I find them unmoved, impatient. I look to Seward: "It is possible I have erred in my supposition?"

Seward's reply is curt: "You have."

"Then I suppose I must only shift my ground of request. Let me ask for this concession. I am content to implore in such a case, not on personal grounds, but for the sake of others. I am not at liberty to give you the whole of my reasons, but you may, I assure you, take it from me that they are good ones, sound and unselfish, and spring from the highest sense of duty. Could you look, sir, into my heart, you would approve to the full the sentiments which animate me."

In contrast with his disinterested companions, Van Helsing continues to regard me with a gaze of concentrated intensity: "Can you not tell frankly your real reason for wishing to be free tonight? I will undertake that if you will satisfy even me, a stranger, without prejudice, and with the habit of keeping an open mind, Doctor Seward will give you, at his own risk and on his own responsibility, the privilege you seek."

Seward purses his lips at this enormous presumption but holds his tongue: a pupil submitting to the will of his teacher. There is no way I can reveal my true motives if I am to have any chances of being set free. What would I say? That a plague is coming, spread by an ancient creature who steals the blood of others to extend his life, turning his victims into beings just like himself? That I am the only person with the power to put a stop to it? They would banish me to a padded cell in an instant. I look at my feet and shake my head.

"Come, sir," continues the Dutchman, "bethink yourself. You claim the privilege of reason in the highest degree, since you seek to impress us with your complete reasonableness. You do this, whose sanity we have reason to doubt, since you are not yet released from medical treatment for this very defect. If you will not help us in our effort to choose the wisest course, how can we perform the duty which you yourself put upon us?"

Hot tears well in my eyes as I feel my opportunity slipping away: "If were free to speak I should not hesitate a moment, but I am not my own master in the matter. I can only ask you to trust me. If I am refused, the responsibility does not rest with me."

Acting on his empathy, Seward tries to bring the grave scene to an end. He gestures to his guests: "Come now, my friends, we have work to do."

"No!" I yell in a burst of furious desperation, racing forward and seeking to obstruct him from the door.

After exchanging glances with Van Helsing he stops and sighs: "Renfield, I can certainly write to the Home Office on your behalf but at present that is all I can promise."

My face is wet now, my tears flowing in heavy drops. The lives of countless others depend on my success. There are those who have already died as a result of my inaction, my cowardliness. I must redeem myself, I must find Lucy, I must put anyone who has been infected out of their misery: this is all true. But mostly I must also bring my own suffering to an end. I must get out of here. I cannot stand to face my master again. If I stay in Carfax, he will come for me: "Let me entreat you, Doctor Seward, let me implore you, to let me out of this place at once. Send me away how you will and where you will, take me in a strait waistcoat, manacled and leg-ironed, even to gaol, but let me go out of this. You don't know what you do by keeping me here. I am speaking from the depths of my heart, of my very soul. You don't know whom you wrong, or how, and I may not tell. I may not tell. By all you hold sacred, by all you hold dear, by your love that is lost, for the sake of the Almighty, take me out of this and save my soul from guilt. Can't you hear me, man? Can't you understand? Will you never learn? Don't you know that I am sane and earnest now, that I am no lunatic in a mad fit, but a sane man fighting for his soul? You must hear me."

The Superintendent stands over me-my fresh-faced counterpart-holding out his hand and waiting patiently for my entreaty to come to a close. Only now do I realise that his guests have left the room and we are alone.

"Come," he says quietly. "No more of this. We have had quite enough already."

With these well-meant words he abandons me to my fate.

✱

The sun dips below the horizon, as it must. This time I leave the shutter open.

A low mist rolls across the fields, reflecting the moonlight in a way that makes it seem more substantial than a vapour, closer to a rising sea. I sit on my chair, I pace the room. Judging by the sounds echoing around the corridors of Carfax my fellow inmates are more agitated than ever. The very walls groan and creak. The building is shifting.

I am not afraid. With my failure comes an unexpected sense of relief. My fate was decided long, long ago and there was nothing to be gained from struggling. If free will exists, if man can chose his own course through life—something I now doubt—then the luxury was never granted to me. Whatever lies ahead, I will accept it.

For the briefest of moments I close my eyes...

When I open them again he is there, his palms pressed against the glass. Wet, bright blood covers his chin and neck, soaking his collar and the lapels of his jacket. His eyes bulge grotesquely. It is a wonder that heaven should tolerate so monstrous an indulgence of the lusts and malignity of hell. He has been feasting tonight.

"Do what you will," I tell him.

Although he looks in my direction he does not see me. He has consumed too much and become too wild, closer to an untamed animal than ever. His head twitches and jerks like a sparrow's, his skin is swollen. He is much younger now, only just an adult. As if acting independently from the rest of his fidgeting body his left forefinger raises and taps against the glass.

"I will let you in," I say, "provided you promise to take only me. Do no harm to anyone else in here."

These words seem to give him some kind of calm and focus. As I approach I see a dark mass spreading across the land towards us, coming on like the shape of a flame of fire, transforming the mist into something rolling, squirming and gleaming. Looking closer I see it has become an orgy of rats and hares, reaching out to the horizon, ten feet deep at least and stinking of life and death. It is intended as a kind of symbol, I think, but I cannot tell what it is meant to represent. Engorged and bloated on power my master has lost himself. Taking one hand from the glass he uses the back of his hand to wipe blood from his chin and licks it hungrily clean. His teeth are sharp as the blades of a trephine.

Beneath him the land is changing shape again. Pushing up through the writhing sea are millions of cats and dogs, some tearing the rats and hares limb from limb and gorging on their guts while others rut and copulate. Attracted by the scent, swarms of flies fill the sky above them, at first gathering into giant humming spheres then dispersing, blacking out the stars. Bats inevitably follow, then barn owls, bewildered by this glut, striking each other mid flight and spinning to their deaths. When the pray on the ground has all been consumed the dogs turn on the cats, shaking them by their necks and flinging them into the air for sport. It is blood and semen and chaos. A red cloud takes over my eyes and before I know what I am doing I find myself lifting the sash.

The sky is clear and the animals are gone, vanished in an instant and replaced by the cool, thick blanket of fog. Though the gap between the window and the frame is only an inch wide my master slips through, just as the moon herself has often come in through the tiniest crack and stood before me in all her size and splendour.

We are close together, almost touching. His odour is dizzyingly rich and foetid, like rotting undergrowth after a storm. If only he would touch me, take me in his arms, he could grant me peace.

I offer him my throat, but he has already forgotten I am here. Tiptoeing, convulsing, searching, he creeps across the floorboards and out of the room.

*

The water pipes clank in the walls. The Irish attendant brings my breakfast.

"You're quiet today."

"I could not sleep."

Outside it is drizzling and the landscape is grey. At mid-morning the sirens are tested. Everything is ordinary, nothing has changed.

I must admit to myself that my motives for inviting my master inside were less noble than I would like to believe. A small part of me hoped submitting to his will would earn me some reward. All day I wait but nothing comes, not even a spider or a blowfly.

If I fight him I am powerless. If I obey him he disregards me. This thought sends me to bed, fully dressed, to fall into a long, deep and dreamless sleep.

When I wake it is raining and Mrs Harker is in the room, sat waiting on my chair and dressed in a grey woollen walking suit with a length of black ribbon around her neck. A strange muted light comes from outside, giving her whole body a yellowish tinge.

"Mr Renfield. I do hope you don't object to me dropping by to see you unannounced."

She is speaking slowly, quietly. I sit up and straighten my clothes: "Not at all. How are you, madam?"

"I'm afraid I my husband has rather abandoned me for the past few days. He is very busy with Doctor Seward."

"I'm sorry to hear that."

"I don't fare well without companionship. Being alone

214

all the time is bad for one's state of mind, don't you agree?"

"You are wise to say so."

The strange light dims, revealing her complexion to be pale and drawn, like tea after the teapot has been watered. The liveliness I detected in her eyes when we first met has all but gone. I ask her if she has been having trouble with her sleep.

"How did you know? Do I look that awful? I have been waking up during the night and having curious dreams. Not frightening, you understand, only somewhat disorienting. Mr Harker assures me they will pass in time. Are you feeling all right, Mr Renfield?"

Ashamed at my burgeoning tears I stand, turn away from the lady and look out of the window. The rain persists and the sky is growing darker.

"I wish I had made more of an effort to speak to you," I say. "I was nervous of saying the wrong things, or of offending you. It seems foolish now."

"When do you mean? The last time I came here?"

"No. When the wind took your parasol, remember? In Regent's Park. It blew into the fountain. I must have looked utterly comical to you, bumbling around trying to retrieve it. What must you have thought of me?"

"You have me mixed up with someone else. I have only been to London once and I have never been to Regent's Park."

"It was a long time ago. You have probably forgotten it. I so wanted to strike up a friendship with you afterwards but I suppose it simply wasn't to be." Try as I might to sustain an illusion of composure my emotion betrays itself in my cracked voice. "I am sorry for what I did to your gentleman friend. Truly."

"I'm afraid I don't know what you mean."

"I wasn't in my right mind. I had been under intolerable pressure, you see. Intolerable. I don't remember the incident. I only know what I have been told: that I attacked him and beat him with a pipe. Whoever did those things, it was not me. It is not in my nature. I was elsewhere, for a while."

"Please don't be upset."

"As for the terrible thing I did to you when we were children, in the woods by the river.... For years I have wanted to tell you how sorry I am, Magdalene. I have carried the secret with me for so long. Shame has infected my mind, twisted it into something grotesque. When I die and they cut open my head I am sure they will find a contorted, ugly, hairy lump, mutated by guilt and unrecognisable as a brain. I wish I could blame my actions on being a confused young boy but my conscience will not allow it. I accept the blame in full. I wish I had been born a different man."

No longer ashamed of my tears I turn to face her.

Outside, the rain has turned to hail, playing the devil's tattoo against the window.

"And now, as if this were not enough, I have exposed you to danger, left you vulnerable to attack yet again, even as I tried to protect you. It is hopeless. I have let him inside."

She is on her feet: "I must go now. It has been good to talk to you."

When reach out to touch the ribbon around her neck she flinches and ducks away. Something falls to the floor: her pearl earring.

"I am sorry for everything, Magdalene. Truly I am."

"My husband will be expecting me."

"If I could just know you forgive me I could find salvation."

"Goodbye, Mr Renfield."

"If I could only hear the words."

"Goodbye."

A flash of lightning, a peal of thunder, and I know that if I am to find absolution I must confront my master for the final time, whatever the cost. I pick up the pearl earring and put it in my pocket.

✳

Later, when night has fallen and my door has been

locked, I hear movement in the corridor: the night watcher's chair scraping along the tiles. I have not changed into my nightclothes or gone back to bed. Instead I have been filling the time I have left by flicking through a book leant to me by Mr Wainwright: a critical study of poems by Coleridge.

A period of silence follows; just long enough for me to believe that my ears have been tricked by the constant background noise of the storm. A small, reddish spider travels across the ceiling.

Then something clicks, the sound, I think, of the door at the end of the corridor being opened and closed, someone coming in or going out.

Footsteps. Slow and steady. Coming towards my room.

I put down the book and straighten my waistcoat and tie. Getting to my feet I prepare myself to face whatever or whoever is waiting outside.

*

It was the summer solstice, the longest day. When I went to my bedroom after a mostly silent supper with my uncle it was still light outside. I could not have slept even if I wanted to, so keyed up was I anticipating the night to come. For most of the day I had confined myself to the disused nursery, pacing back and forth in my stockinged feet, teaching myself how to walk while making as little noise as possible.

I waited for half an hour before retrieving the paring knife I had stolen from the kitchen. A few moments later I lifted the mattress again and put it back where it had been resting for the past three nights. Was I really going to go through with what I had planned? Once the deed was done there would be no undoing it. After a period of stasis-my will to act battling against my doubts and leaving me in a state where I could do nothing but stare at the floor-I made my decision and began to undress.

With my outer clothes draped over the bed's footrest I took the knife out again and inserted the blade's tip into the top of the seam that ran down the side of my leather corset. By working it back and forth for a few minutes I was able to cut the first tight loop of cotton thread before moving down to the next one, then the next. It was an activity that caused me a great deal of discomfort, requiring me to keep my arms raised at an awkward angle and my neck twisted. By the time half of the seam had been unpicked the job became much easier and I was able to pull the material apart using my strength alone. My discomfort was not at an end, though. Foolishly I had imagined that after freeing my torso I would be able to slip the metal waist band off without much effort. In practice it jammed over my hipbones and required me to lie on the floor, rocking from side to side and forcing it down in increments, scraping off my top layer of skin in the process. Squeezing it over my thighs was just as difficult. When I was finally rid of the garment I hid it in the base of my wardrobe. How I would explain all this to Mrs Highsmith and my uncle when washday came around I did not know. My intention was to steal a needle and thread to repair it myself but I knew this would be difficult. For now, I needed to get dressed and focus on the task at hand. Reasoning that I might need protection if I was about to go into the countryside at nightfall, I slipped the knife into my jacket pocket.

The only way down to the ground floor took me directly past Uncle Patrick's study. While I was no longer young or naïve enough to truly believe wishing for something would make it happen, a part of me still sincerely hoped that simply by willing it I could make it so he had already gone to bed. If I were to be caught I could only imagine the severity of the punishment I would be dealt. Carrying my shoes in one hand I crept onto the landing and saw that the study was still occupied and the door was ajar. How I found the courage to walk by I do not know—I was light-headed and my heart was thumping against my ribs—but I managed to pass without detection and descend the stairs.

I waited until I was outside before I put my shoes on.

The sun was in the lower quarter of the sky and the air was cooling. The moment my laces were tied I set off at a run.

Despite my athleticism I was out of breath by the time I came in sight of the row of cottages, less brilliantly white now the end of the day was drawing near. I had run what I reckoned was two and a half miles and set off at far too fast a pace. Bent over with my hands resting on my knees - regulating my breath and wondering whether I would be spotted and sent home – I gathered my strength before starting again, this time at a more maintainable speed.

By the time I was running down the slope which signalled the end of the route the temperature had taken another dip. Soon the light would begin to fade. Pausing, I scanned the scene ahead: the fence stile, the distant bridge, the edge of the woods. There was no sign of Magdalene. I cursed myself for forgetting to bring a watch. There was no way of telling if I was too early or, God forbid, too late. Was she yet to arrive or had she already gone home? Climbing the stile I resolved to wait for as long as was necessary.

This interval gave me time to reflect, which did me no good. Sat on the bridge's low parapet I imagined what might be going on at home. Had Uncle Patrick come to check on me and found me missing? Was he, even now, pulling the torn corset out of my wardrobe and holding it up in front of himself, just as I had on the night he first gave it to me? As my body relaxed my fear increased. Perhaps my uncle would disown me, send me back to Ceylon—or wherever my father was now—as a lost cause. Was it worth it?

Just then I caught sight of a figure walking across the grassy field: Magdalene, singing quietly to herself with the setting sun at her back, wearing the same white dress she wore on the day of the flying ants. Her journey towards me seemed to take an age. Waiting for her on the cold stone I told myself her approach was an image I would carry with me for the rest of my days.

Once she was close enough I dismounted and, unsure how to greet her away from the supervision of adults, performed a deep bow. That she laughed at me and responded with a theatrical curtsy wounded my pride a little, but her smile made it easy to forgive.

She confessed she had worried that I wouldn't come.

"Of course I came."

"I thought you might hate me."

"Hate you? No, not at all. Never. Why would I hate you?"

"For getting you into trouble. Because of what I did. Did your uncle punish you?"

"No. In fact he never mentioned it."

She looks bemused: "My father told me he had

forbidden us from seeing each other again."

"Of course. I meant he hasn't mentioned any other punishment. Sorry, I didn't express myself very well."

"Well, I'm happy you're here."

Without discussing it further we set off over the bridge and crossed the path, into the woods.

"How did you get out of the house?" she asked.

"It was easy. I jumped out of my bedroom window. I learned how to land properly when I was in Ceylon so I didn't hurt myself."

"What will happen if you're found out?"

"I don't care if I'm found out. Uncle Patrick doesn't scare me. He's not my father."

She ducked under a low hanging branch and I followed. Soon we came across the broad tree close to the steep ravine then, farther on, the ditch where we had discovered the half-eaten hare. Without warning she stopped and kissed me on the lips, before turning away and heading deeper into the woods. That she had her back to me was a relief. Her actions had triggered a physical reaction and I was worried it would be noticed. For the first time I wondered why I had come, and why she asked me.

The foliage was becoming thicker and less easy to negotiate. Branches cracked under our feet; a wood pigeon cooed at intervals. Night was coming. Patting my jacket I checked I was still carrying my knife. Magdalene reached out and took my hand in hers.

Happening across a small clearing we halted again. This time she did not kiss me but stared wide-eyed at something ahead.

"What's wrong?"

In the dying light, in a patch of brambles and half shrouded by mist, stood a man covered from head to toe in dirt. His suit was torn and there were scratches on his hands and face. Lifting his head he stared directly at us and, for a moment, I thought it might be my father. Magdalene panicked and turned on her heels, darting back amongst the trees. I looked again. Now it seemed there was no man at all, only shadows, twigs and leaves. Could it have been an optical illusion? Too unsettled to find out I ran after my companion.

She was more adept at moving through the woodland than I expected and had soon gained a substantial lead. I called for her to slow down but she paid no heed, her dress hitched up to her thighs as she pushed through the branches. It was not long before I lost sight of her completely. The daylight was fading fast. Knowing it was no good to keep up the chase I stopped and called again, all the time expecting to feel the hand of the wild man falling heavily on my shoulder. A reply came in the form of a crash beyond a fallen tree up ahead. Preying it was not the sound of a pursuer I set off in its direction.

After I vaulted the trunk the ground seemed to give way beneath my feet. Mercifully I was able to catch hold of a sturdy branch that stuck out to my side and stop myself from tumbling forward. I found myself at the edge of the deep ravine, overlooking the bed of ivy-clustered rocks below. Some way down and to the left, in a spot that was now only just visible, I caught sight of an unnatural white shape: Magdalene, her limbs oddly splayed and her head hanging back. She must have lost her footing and fallen.

Everything was silent. There was no doubt now I would be found out by my uncle. Magdalene would return home filthy and injured and be forced to confess. Tightening my hand around the damp bark I saw only one option open to me.

Even as I fled I was ashamed. Giving little thought to the direction in which I was headed I dumbly contemplated the scale of the betrayal I was committing. I was abandoning my friend, leaving her alone and exposed, defenceless against an attack. But however strong my feelings of guilt they could not combat the compulsion to run. Finding an unfamiliar dirt track I followed it in hope it might lead me to the bridge. Instead I emerged onto an elevated road from where I could see the red pillar box. This time I was able to sprint the rest of the way home without stopping.

*

Of course, I had known she might be dead. In the woods I was unable to admit the possibility to myself but back at home, lying in bed, it was all I could think of: her broken body on the rocks, rain water filling her nostrils and her mouth. Over and over I told myself I was overreacting-that she had probably struggled to her feet and made it home to Oscar, furious with me but alive at least—but try as I might, I did not believe it.

My corset was where I left it, my absence was undiscovered. The storm arrived with the dawn and went on until breakfast when I heard the clicking of my uncle's cane as he tackled the stairs. In the dining room I methodically consumed everything on my plate, despite my nausea. If Patrick noticed my washed out pallor and my restrained fidgeting he made no mention of it, preferring instead to confidently impart more wisdom from his book on boy's health. After we had eaten I declared I was going into the garden to read and he shuffled away to his office.

I made my escape over the hedge behind the oak tree where I had buried Magdalene's letter, then rounded the house through the neighbouring fields. I travelled to the woods at a walking pace, telling myself that there was nothing to be concerned about and therefore no need to hurry. In truth I was delaying my arrival, scared of what I would find.

When I reached the bridge my shoes were soaked from crossing the field. The river was swollen and moving fast, farther up the bank than I had ever seen it before. I entered the wood at the usual spot and retraced our steps. Locating the fallen tree was easier than I imagined, taking only a matter of minutes. Before looking into the ravine I hesitated and considered turning back. Might it be better not to know the truth? Don't be so childish, I told myself. She won't be there. She will have gone home.

But she was there. Her sodden dress clung tight to her body, her spine arched over the sharp rocks. One leg was twisted back on itself. The blood had gone from her, leaving her skin glistening and silvery like the wings of a moth. Feeding at her throat was a wild dog with patchy fur and prominent ribs, its snout pressed deep under her chin. All around heavy drops of rain water were falling from the trees, striking the blanket of leaves with a popping sound, like finger snaps or the clucking of a tongue. Released by the storm the rich stench of rotting vegetation filled the air.

Sensing my presence the dog turned its dark eyes towards me and bristled before pelting up the side of the ravine and away into the bushes. When I was sure it had gone I found a place where I could climb down, slipping once and dirtying my coat at the elbows. Having no means

227

to dig a grave I spent the next few hours searching for loose rocks and clambering around the side of the ravine to collect heavy branches, my clothes growing steadily dirtier as I did so. Each time I moved away from the corpse a sparrow fluttered down to peck around the edges of the dress, flying away again when I returned. Unable to look any longer at Magdalene's lifeless face I covered it first, placing pebbles over her eyes and the blade of a fern across her throat.

Only when the body was completely concealed did I begin the long journey back to my uncle's house. The snapping sound of the rainwater striking the undergrowth echoed in my ears; the ripe smell of the vegetation clung to my filthy clothes, stuck to my skin, so that I thought I might never be able to wash it away.

.... VAN Helsing dips his handkerchief into the carafe and wrings out the excess water before gently running it over Renfield's bruised and tender face. Seward crouches at his patient's side while Morris leans against the wall and pulls at the side of his moustache, tired and becoming bored. Godalming, in his greatcoat and nightgown, observes from the chair. It is raining hard.

"When he came tonight I was ready for him," says the patient. "I saw the mist stealing in and I grabbed it tight. I had heard that madmen have unnatural strength and as I knew I was a madman, at times anyhow, I resolved to use my power. And he felt it too, for he had to come out of the mist and take human form. I held tight and I thought I was going to win till I saw his eyes. They burned into me, and my strength became like water. He slipped through it, and when I tried to cling to him he raised me up and flung me down."

A few seconds pass between a lightning strike and its accompanying crack of thunder. The storm is moving away.

"Seward," he says, and the Superintendent takes his hand. "He is here, inside the asylum. You must save her.

229

It's too late for me."

"I will."

"You must promise it."

He makes the promise, although he doesn't understand.

Van Helsing lays the handkerchief on the tray: "There's nothing more we can do for him. At least we have been able to make him comfortable."

The patient's eyelids are growing heavy. They flicker as he struggles to keep them open: "Seward," he says, swallowing dryly and passing his tongue over his lips: "Make sure you tell her I tried my best."

Somewhere in the distance he can hear waves lapping against a shore and, quite distinctly, the call of a Ceylon Lorikeet.

"Of course. Don't worry. Everything will be fine."

A steady breeze blows in from the Indian Ocean. Giggling girls play happily on the sand. Bright sunshine warms his face. He is going home.

"It is important," he says, or doesn't say.

ACKNOWLEDGEMENTS

Thanks to Layla Vandenbergh for her invaluable assistance with the manuscript.

The cover image was originally taken from Guillaume-Benjamin-Amand Duchenne de Boulogne's *The Mechanism of Human Physiology* (1862). Thanks to Dan Waters for designing the jacket.

This book could not have been written without the support, encouragement, patience and generosity of Martha Waters. Cheers, Boog!

"You're the best! Around! Nothing's gonna ever keep you down…"

2792611R00127

Printed in Great Britain
by Amazon.co.uk, Ltd.,
Marston Gate.